Tart, *with* a Silken Finish

Tart, *with* a Silken Finish

Peter Barthelme

St. Martin's Press

New York

Library of Congress Cataloging-in-Publication Data

Barthelme, Peter.
    Tart, with a silken finish / by Peter Barthelme.
       p. cm.
     ISBN 0-312-01832-0
     I. Title.
     PS3552.A7633T3 1988   87-38241
813'.54—dc19   CIP

10 9 8 7 6 5 4 3 2

to Uncle Don and Uncle Rick,
with love

Tart, *with* a Silken Finish

SHE WAS NOT *REALLY* WORTHLESS, I guess, nobody is, right?

People have a certain magic, inalienable rights, intrinsic value, or so I had been trained/had trained myself to think. Yet Margrit gave every indication of being right on the border of just plain no-count as my friends at the bay would say. She was behind on her rent, even after I gave her the money twice, being dunned by half a dozen other creditors, and her career was sidetracked for the moment. The moment had been four months now but a figure model had to pick her spots or she gets treated like trash I was told. Time was against her, in any case. Against us all but hers was a stronger vulnerability. She lied to herself, not to mention me. She demanded tangibles and gave occasional lust, although lust, in theory at least, was what I was after. Or was I? What I told myself and the way I felt often were at odds. Margrit was a tall and streaky blonde and I missed the doorway and walked into the wall—literally—the first time I saw her.

I envied her.

She was a girl, to start with, and with contrarian logic I still thought that carried certain advantages, despite the fact I had been educated to the accompanying difficulties too. And she seemed untroubled by any thought other than how to get her hands on, what? Assets, charge accounts, money, prestige, "A" lists?

I envied her ability, honed to a sharp edge, of surmounting every fear and doubt that she had, and that she had them I was certain since it was to me that she came to resolve her problems. Yet she could manage to blank off all inhibiting higher-being thoughts and move with unself-conscious grace and—eyes slitted, mouth pursed—devote herself strictly to the animal, without any inhibitions whatsoever.

She fucked like a rabbit. Scary.

I was in an excellent position to observe this since she was straddling my naked body, using what remained of my manhood to get herself one more climax. We both had been there but she wasn't finished. She leaned over to kiss me briefly, nipples hard against my chest, and whispered that she liked me because with me she could be as "dirty as she wanted." Then she moved up to press against my mouth and I went to work. The alternative was to smother. Her waist was lean, her rib cage just barely visible under smooth flesh, and I was failing to keep up with my part of the fantasy, damnit. I could hear my dog, Bullit, scratching a flea from her position by the door.

I was late for a meeting.

I was frequently late for meetings and some were taking place without me. I was also going broke at an accelerating rate and as much as I would have liked to blame Margrit for these things, I was forced to accept responsibility for both as well as all my *other* actions and I cursed Hector Edfelter for lifting my masterfully created bullshit curtain, there in his carefully decorated, no-offense, shrink-style office at $110 an hour. As my mind wandered, I wilted and caused Margrit to renew her clever efforts with just the tips of her fingers, clear no-polish polish on the nails, strong, workman's hands at the end of slender arms. She gave up on me, ground strongly against my mouth, shuddered briefly, and rolled off, enabling my first good breath for the past several eternities. My lip hurt.

"Want me to . . ." she said, gesturing.

I rolled over, hiding the offending member, and said, "Not to worry. Another time. I'm old, you know."

She fell back on the pillows and lit a cigarette, idly tweaking her dark brown nipples and smiling. I hoped I had been satisfactory. It was a hope that was becoming increasingly forlorn and once more I vowed to do something about her. Depletion leads to logic. She was supposed to disagree with the "old" crack.

I called the office from the kitchen and spoke to Tammy, my sweet young secretary and she-who-lies-for-the-boss. While she read the list of calls and recited urgent messages, threats in several cases, I wondered how I managed to get quite as fucked up as I had. Infatuation was a young man's disease.

Conversely, if I insisted on being infatuated, why couldn't I manage to ignore reality in the carefree manner of my naked friend in the bedroom? It's hell being half saint/half sinner. I visualized myself, standing in the sunbright kitchen, a touch paunchy if I forgot to suck in my gut, balding not bald, two fingers gone on the left hand, a commentary on my failure to keep hands out of leader wire when boating large fish. In the mirror, I automatically held my head for the most attractive reflection.

I asked Tammy to call the bank downtown, where I

was supposed to be, and explain that I had a personal emergency and would call in as soon as it was solved. Then I took the personal emergency into the shower and washed it gingerly.

When I got out, Margrit was already dressed, cool and composed, and she laughed when she saw me in the suit. "Come here," she said, and held my face to the light. She took out her makeup kit and applied something to my upper lip.

"This way you can tell everybody it's razor burn," she said, and kissed my nose. Then she "borrowed" another forty bucks, all I had on me, and rattled off in her old VW bug. I didn't know where she was going and I was afraid to ask.

By the time I got back to the agency it was very nearly too late to do anything and Tammy had a reproving expression. She didn't like Margrit, no woman did, and a lunch that lasted till four-twenty was not approved of in the marketing classes that had composed the bulk of her exposure to the advertising business. She gave me a stack of pink message slips and waited by the desk while I leafed through them.

"Okay," I said. "I can take care to these tomorrow. What about the bank?"

"Mr. Tuckerman said to call him today or forget it," she said. "Then he slammed the phone."

"Damn," I said, "he must think a half-million-dollar budget gives him some clout." I waved her out and mouthed "Thank you" as I dialed the number.

"Hey," I said when he came on the line. "I'm sorry. Something came up."

"Beaumont, you're dealing with people who are unaccustomed to being jacked around and you're making me look foolish for recommending you. For our advertising." I knew what for.

"I know, I'm sorry, it couldn't be avoided."

"We've postponed the presentation for a week, I managed that much. But that's it. No more excuses, no more missed meetings."

"I could do it tomorrow," I lied.

"I want it in a week. Same time, same place."

And he hung up. This was to tell me he was pissed. I had taken him fishing once and his fishing clothes were pressed. He was a tiny little man, even in the brain. Weasel or ferret, depending on my mood. Mousse on the too-thick brown hair. Slept in a suit, a sleeping suit, Neiman-Marcus. Once every month or so, he dropped by and shyly inquired if I could get him some coke, hinting about big billing on the horizon. I always begged off, somewhat stiff, worried, and then supplied him with a phone number. It made me feel pimp-y. I thought the white stuff vastly overrated anyway, preferring bourbon.

I wondered what the hell I was going to create for him. Bank advertising bored me stiff and I was sure that bank ads had the same effect on the reader.

For some hundreds of years banks had solemnly got money at tiny rates and lent it out at outrageous ones and crushed any outsider who was a nanosecond late in paying. This was called fiscal responsibility and bankers wore it like a cloak. Somehow, the banking lobby had grown so fat and so somnolent that deregulation had reared its ugly head. It put them in a pickle, since they were the first to preach free market values. Faced with their own free market, and competition from Sears et al, they wished to yell and holler for support from somewhere but their dignity forbade it. So, with stiff upper lips firmly in place, bankers watched their institutions fail like crazy through the eighties trailing only the S&Ls, who had always been rather a poor relation anyhow.

I was supposed to fix all that with advertising. For a downtown bank that had no discernable power base, no clique of friends and money sources who could be fattened with special loans and insider tips, and who would in turn direct more friends to bring their money to give to the bank which would then lend it out to more friends and an occasional foolhardy consumer who had better watch his ass.

I had assured them it was possible. Now they wanted results. Even their parking was overpriced, I thought gloomily. The analogy with Margrit was inescapable and I poured myself a staggering drink to think it over while Tammy tidied her desk before going home. Nothing really new had appeared in bank advertising in many a moon. Generally, something new—however promising—was regarded by clients with the fond admiration they reserved for scorpions in the bedroll, anyway.

I wonder where Margrit was headed in the VW?

I NEVER MEANT TO GET MIDDLE-AGED. Sometimes, sweaty from my efforts on the racquetball court, I even forgot I was, every muscle oiled by frenetic exertion and the sneaky-good feeling of destroying my opponent bubbling through my veins.

I would know it the next morning, when the adrenaline was gone.

I knew it now, sitting at my desk with absolutely nothing I really wanted to do. Nothing. Not ads, not drinking, not friends, nothing I really wanted. I was middle-aged, saturated. Perhaps that was the real reason I put up with an alcoholic would-be figure model whose major contribution to society was to keep the credit machinery, collection division, in good working order. Margrit inspired strong emotions even while I thought bad things about her.

If I was critical of Margrit, what about myself? I financed her and missed out on the benefits, by and large, and had been known to burst out in tears when my late-night amateur investigations showed she was once more chasing tail. Or whatever the female equivalent of that noble sport may be. Always richer and more rewarding in fantasy, why did it hurt so much when she was thus engaged?

Margrit, at least, enjoyed her pretensions. And she still lusted: after money, after power, after intimate little dinners with important people, after a new car. The fact that any or all of the above was available to her through application and work was a concept she wished not to discuss. She had successfully managed to while away enough years so that she needed some sort of shortcut to wealth, a rich husband the route of choice. Because I had some limited entree into circles where she fondly imagined such potential husbands hung out, I was a useful escort.

She had a mean streak of self-hatred working too, enough so that she frequently managed to disgrace herself in the social company of Potential Husbands, which was the way I thought of them. Throwing up in the backseat of a Mercedes was not the way to win friends and influence proposals.

Perhaps at one point she put me into the Potential category too, although *that* was a mistake I would not make again. "I could do so much with your house. Little gatherings for important people . . ." she would confide, and I would blanch.

God, she made me feel alive though, poor performance not withstanding. She was ornamental and I liked that, of course, preening a bit. Her continued presence was a rebuttal to all the things I feared. I burned for the years to fall away from me, as they did on the racquetball court, and I learned her sexual secrets thoroughly, not enjoying myself that much, grim and determined to make up in application what I lacked in youth and trimness and animal lust. I was a crafty bastard if nothing else and always willing to work.

I would ask her about her lovers' techniques and abilities, desperate to know and masking my urgencies with false bravado, offering to trade war stories, needing a rank order in which to place myself. She coyly refused to come through with facts, although she must have had enough to reassure/alarm several people like me. I didn't expect overt honesty but felt that I could glean the truth from the cracks and crevices of her lies. Sodium Pentothal sounded wonderful.

I could see her in my mind, quick strides to the office door as the rusty VW groaned and tinkled after her heedless driving, coming to see me with a sly smile, a twisting around the fingertips was all, more money, an appointment, would I like to leave? Every once in a while, she'd do or say something so out-of-context wonderful, it would make me stare, a cutting comment here, a delightful gesture there. Her skin had no pores, I'd swear to it. She showed me how impotent my precious ratiocinations were, dry beliefs and arid posturings melting in the light of her physical presence and frenetic style.

"Don't talk, don't think, *do* it," she snapped.

Maybe she had gone to an interview or something useful.

"So what brilliance have you for the bank, dummy?" I said aloud. I scrunched up in the chair, a posture tough to achieve when one has acres of legs to fold up. I felt comforted by it and there was no one to see.

One competitor touted its people and another its data processing, one claimed to be *the* bank for Texas and another bragged about its contribution to Houston. Still another used a canned program, a syndicated advertising campaign that saved them the cost of making the ads and filled ad agency people like myself with greedy despair.

It was an ugly campaign and the flat accentless tones of the announcer betrayed its syndicated past. But did anyone notice, that was the rub.

I took a black-covered sketch pad from the desk and started drawing, not a bad diversion for a writer who detested the amiable brown tones of the IBM Selectric sitting in the corner on the butcher block desk. I drew circles for a while and played the game of making an X and seeing how closely I could bisect it with one swift line drawn from the far corner.

What did people want from a bank? Money? Not really, I thought, what did *I* want from a bank? I thought back to my first transactions, the first car loan, the first of several consolidation loans. Financial advice could be found in more depth in the columns of the newspaper or certainly *Forbes*, so what did I want?

I flashed to the confessional and the peculiar wooden way it would smell, there at St. Anne's, Fridays at two-thirty, desperate and deciding which sins were acceptable and which should be buried, hoping to get them included in a blanket absolution and not the prying priest this time, please, rather a religious lottery that. Absolution, that's what we want from our financial cathedrals.

I uncoiled and walked to the sneering typewriter, flicked its switch, and typed, "IT'S OKAY." Then I turned it off. Got to save electricity, HL&P could get nasty quick.

I went back to the sketch pad and drew a little oblong like a newspaper ad in miniature and put "IT'S OKAY" at the top and propped the pad against the wall to stare at it.

I'd read that.

I felt the trickle starting and I went back to the Selectric and turned it on again and began to write an ad, feeling the flow and liking it because this I knew how to do, did it better than most and more consistently than anybody, and that *was* worth something if only to me.

The ad started out like this: IT'S OKAY. Then, smaller:

WHATEVER IT IS. NOT BECAUSE WE'RE SUCH GOOD GUYS, AL-
THOUGH WE ARE, BUT BECAUSE WE NEED YOU MORE THAN
YOU NEED US. Paragraph. THIS REALIZATION MAY STUN THE
BANKING WORLD, BUT IT'S THE TRUTH. SO WE *WANT* TO SAY,
"IT'S OKAY." IT'S OUR FAVORITE PHRASE, NO MATTER WHAT
THE PROJECT. Paragraph. You get the general drift. The
words whipped out of my brain, through the fingers into
the typewriter, damn the typos and spelling, and I had the
campaign.

I was a bit surprised.

Before I was through, I had the bones and a good bit of
flesh: newspaper, outdoor (I hated billboards but they
were a useful method of intruding into the customer's
consciousness), magazine, some in-bank stuff, a nice
statement stuffer, and broadcast media. I could see the
whole thing and what I had was a pile of scribbles, some
headlines typed on yellow paper and body copy for the
stuffer. Not bad for an old fart. It was dark outside now.

I locked up the office, which was a converted two-story
house in a mixed-use neighborhood, now mostly popu-
lated by Vietnamese, one of whom had the disquieting
habit of squatting on a corner for hours watching everything. He wore a crisp green officer's jacket over never-
changing blue shorts and would at times return a friendly
nod. I always wondered what he'd seen and how he got
to the street corner, this street, in Houston. My building
was comfy, hardly cutting edge, but it beat twelve hundred square feet one corner office fourteen floors up. I
kept the art department, presently without artist, upstairs,
with an expensive stat camera and enough press-down
letters to publish a book. Maybe someday the office will
be worth what I paid for it, should Houston recover.

I went home and when I pulled into the garage I could
see the the neighbor lady standing in the alleyway that
separated our homes. Hers was bigger, more opulent, and
she kept the lawn mowed. I waved hello and she ran

awkwardly toward me, pregnant again, third kid on the way. She had endeared herself to me by excusing herself and her quiet husband from an interminable block party a year ago on the grounds that she "was in heat." I was the only person who laughed at her joke. Lumbering across the alleyway, she was dressed in baggy white rich-people shorts and a maternity top which I'm sure was considered fetching, in the store.

"Somebody's in my house," she whispered when she came near, hands pressing against her bulging stomach. "I could see them through the bathroom window."

"Have you called the cops?"

"I just saw them, go look!"

I didn't want to look or get involved but I was obviously a better choice than she. A century and a half of Texas tradition, killing your own snakes, stirred somewhat sluggishly in my blood. I took her in my dark house, locked the door behind her with instructions to call the police, and ventured forth, a reluctant hero at best, through the cedar fence which surrounded her lot. Her burglar bars, a necessity in our high-rent district, were torn from the hinges and I started rummaging through the miscellaneous batch of tools her husband kept in the garage for a weapon. I was glad to see his garage was as messy as mine.

Bullit, following me curiously, suddenly and loudly went nuts, fluffed up and growling, a let-me-at-them brag. I wasn't so sure I wanted to go inside and view the devastation but the door was indisputably open. I let Bullit go and she raced to the door, howling a surprisingly menacing howl, considering her size. I went to follow, only stopping when I noticed a loud-colored shirt vaguely visible, mostly color, through the frosted glass of the bathroom window. You'd think your average burglar would have more sense than to press up against the window, even a frosted window, although the racket Bullit was making could have destroyed normal burglar thought patterns. He should have turned off the light before he hid in there and I could see him dashing for shelter, eyes wide, mouth open, forgetting to flick the switch or worse remembering it and missing and fearing to go back.

I selected from the motley array of tools in the garage, a two-pound small-shaft sledgehammer in my hand, in a sudden rage. Bullit was in my neighbor's hall, ears flattened back, coat ruffed up to twice her size, snapping and snarling and barking up a storm. It was an impressive display and I paused to get around her, second, third, and fourth thoughts jangling in my tired old brain.

Was I *that* mad or was I playing another role?

In the words of Edfelter, what did I *really* want?

I looked again at the red-painted steel head of the sledgehammer and visualized it against a skull, any skull, even just a tap, and felt the hard hollow thunk of a bump on the brain and wondered if I really wanted to do that to another person, even the person who was presently inhabiting the neighbor's bath. I thought about missing his head too, why deny it, and his likely reactions. Bullit was not so inhibited, even bolder now that I was there, and I dropped the sledge to the floor with a crash that made me glad I hadn't hit anybody and turned to race outside again, confusing the poor dog.

Three steps and I returned to pick up the weapon because I didn't want it used against me and I zipped outside, tossed the sledge into the bushes, and raced to my house. Neighbor-lady was on the phone, eyes flashing with the righteous frightened anger of someone being robbed. She probably visualized worse, assuming the perpetrators were not turned off by swollen bellies.

"You're right," I said inanely. "Are they coming?"

She nodded and I went outside in shame and almost groaned about the cliché, because two young Chicano boys were rounding the corner of the garage, having somehow got past the loud hallway sentry. If they had hurt Bullit, I wished I hadn't had second thoughts about the sledge. I went to confront them, both small and looking scared, or maybe annoyed—who can tell?—noting that one had his shirt rolled up from the bottom, showing a lean brown belly, bastard, and the other was wearing a new sports coat. It was far too big for the little shit. I went for them, pulling up when I saw the carving knife, a fillet blade like I had on the boat, stuck in the hip pocket of the one with the coat.

I was cool, by God I was proud of my cool: "Better run, the cops are on their way." Hard smile.

They mumbled something and I forced them to part to pass me, pivoting and poised to leap away from the knife, them mumbling something and all I heard was "Man?" They walked, then jogged and broke into a run before the end of the block, disappearing around the corner and I was determined not to let them vanish—who me, Officer?—and so ran back to my car, Bullit appearing in a scramble to be with me and making me open the door to let her aboard. We backed out with a screech and turned the corner, all that was lacking was a rooftop light like Kojak, and saw the kids turning another corner two blocks down. The little creeps could move, that was a fact. I felt a little guilt, the two of them together were barely larger than I, and I found myself inventing standard rationalizations for them, deprived childhood, diminished expectations, whatever. Should I have let them steal the TV? Might warp the neighbor's baby.

I got to the corner as fast as a Corvette can move and turned it gently, not knowing what I'd find. They were a block or so away, one with the sports coat over his shoulder and the shirt rolled down on the other one. Were they smart enough to change the image? I idled down the residential street, garbage day in a steel-sack neighborhood, nothing but the best, and followed them.

Say what you will, Houston's Finest earned their pay and more, for we hadn't gone three blocks when I saw the blue 'n white come barreling down the street toward me. This was not lost on my friends who rounded into a side street hastily and I gunned my car across to cut off the oncoming cop, jumped out waving, and watched him nicely execute a panic stop, just this side of sliding the tires for max deceleration. Good guy.

I ran up with my empty hands conspicuously visible and said, "I called it in. You're here about the robbers?"

He nodded a yes and I pointed where they'd gone, stammering a brief description but making sure to say "Latins" when I described the boys, hoping that was the proper, no-prejudice term to use. The policeman nodded, yanked the car around in a tight, over-the-curb circle, and took off with radio microphone in hand. I went back to my car and followed, feeling at last I had found my calling.

3

We caught them, by God, one small blow for justice and paying lots of property taxes. My house turned into headquarters and I made coffee. How the cops swarmed my house! Motorcycle cops and young cops blond and acting tough, more blue 'n whites, all making much out of calling me "Sir" and talking tough cop-talk out of tight-lip mouths, and I remembered nervously my dope stash was in the bedroom. The neighbor-lady kissed me and her hastily summoned husband shook my hand. The phone rang in the midst of all this cop stuff, taking a statement from me, can-you-identify so forth, and Margrit needed picking up because the VW had cratered once more, would I hurry, she was being eyed.

Probably out of gas.

I hated to leave the excitement, feeling a moderate

amount of heroism, but excused myself with pretended, aw-shucks grace. Margrit was drunk and unimpressed and wanted me to take her home but I insisted on checking and a gas can from the station solved her problem. I made her follow me and drove back home, all clear.

During the night's fights I was tempted to ask the neighbor-lady in to testify on my behalf, but managed to resist.

"You know what they got?" I said to sweet Tammy the next morning, noting that I ached all over. Had Margrit been getting in some licks while I slept? Tammy's hair, all spiky in proper punk style, wiggled when she turned to face me. Margrit was still asleep at my house, or possibly going through old love letters.

"They got some change, from a jar, and a lighter that didn't work. The cops made them give back the coat."

"It makes you you feel violated," she said wisely, and I started to argue but thought conventional wisdom was probably accurate enough and I nodded and went back to my sketches and headlines and bursts of body copy to see if my bank campaign had stood the test of time. Advertising is fleeting and overnight is seasoning enough for most of it and that was my normal routine. Tammy to the contrary, I felt rather proud, excited maybe, their house was hardly messed up and I didn't get hurt, burglary interruptus, fixed their ass. And the neighbor-lady kissed very nicely.

I liked the campaign.

That meant it would probably be hard to sell, needed watering down to be acceptable in banking circles. I would argue that banking circles were not the spheres we wished to influence but probably to no avail. I'd call Kennie, the drunk artist, and see if he were working today.

He was and I explained the thing to him, gave him the headlines and a two-day deadline, which was what you needed if you were to work successfully with him. With all his flaws, he'd give me what I needed if I were to sell the idea, slick-looking layouts, mounted and matted and ready to impress, sprayed with clear fix to deepen the blacks and smooth out minor roughness. Oh, they'd be slick and I felt eager for a moment, once more visualizing the gratitude of the client and the awards dinner where I'd pick up another plaque or medal to go with the ones that hung around the office.

The campaign, if accepted, would do a lot to keep my tiny agency in business and I was glad I liked it. I'd probably be able to sell it, fueled by enthusiasm, inspired by both financial need and ego. I waited for the layouts impatiently. The major trauma of the next two days was Bullit annoying the gays who lived next door by chasing their cat. I explained it was difficult to keep a dog, even a peaceful and civilized dog, from chasing cats but they were unimpressed. "Kitty doesn't hurt anything," they said in unison. How could I argue? I promised to do better.

I didn't hear from Margrit, which was strange.

She didn't answer her phone and she didn't come by and her apartment was dark when I drove by a couple of times. I had no claims but I spent hours visualizing her in every sexual permutation and configuration possible, each one more bizarre than the last. We had no strings, I'd made that clear in self-protection but I couldn't stop the panic-anxiety swelling in my guts.

Kennie's layouts were all that I had hoped and more and I was raring to go, good suit laid out, sincere tie in order, latest marketing catchwords at my fingertips. "IT'S OKAY" I would say to Tammy at every available opportunity and watch for her smile. On the brink of a presentation, all else fades.

The bank had decided to go with Traditional Reassuring and the offices were all rosewood and drapes, dark and thickly carpeted, with some stuff on the ceiling that soaked up any nervy sound that had the gall to enter. I had trouble because it was like being in a speaker enclosure and I couldn't decide if I was talking too loud or what. Oh, the bankers were a joke!

The Head Banker had on a beautiful suit of dark English wool, just the faintest stripe, cool white face and cooler blue eyes. He never changed expression, refused to react to my jokes, and hardly seemed to breathe. A spare and elegant man, arrogance dipping from his skin, important messages whispered in his ear, a breathless pause while we waited for him to speak. I wanted badly for him to fart.

All the other bankers were varying carbons of the Head Banker, suits not quite so nice, expressions not quite so cold, no matter how hard they tried, including my old and dear friend Tuckerman who watched my presentation gyrations with an aloof stare which I suspect he practiced in the mirror. Wonder if he'd like to discuss his favorite brand of nose-candy right about now? I should have told them the whole campaign was his idea.

I finished all the reasons why this campaign would revolutionize their business and make their wives passionate once more and paused dramatically: "Gentlemen, that's it. And, if I may say so, IT'S OKAY!"

Then I sat down and stared at the Head Banker, Bechman, determined to force him to nod or smile or something. He tented his hands, manicured fingernails of course, doctor's hands, and reflected. Actually, in context, it would be more accurate to say he Reflected. All the other bankers did so too. When the reflective silence pressed too hard on me I realized I was supposed to be intimidated and it was working and that made me mad. I remembered an old ad agency legend and got up straight-faced to pack away the layouts. They continued to Reflect heavily.

I hefted the portfolio with layouts and stood at the end of the long conference table, seeing my reflection in polished rosewood. I decided I hated rosewood.

"Gentlemen," I said. They looked at me blankly. "Thank you for your valuable time." I headed for the door.

The only thing that spoiled my exit was the zipper on the portfolio case, scratching rosewood a bit when I slid it off the table and I decided to ignore that and them. I wanted to sneak a glance at the Head Banker to see if this would ruffle his starched face but decided against it.

I had my hand on the knob when he cleared his throat.

4

EVEN A BLIND HOG FINDS AN ACORN
now and again and the stars were right for I think I startled even the Head Banker. Tuckerman virtually had a heart attack I'm sure, seeing his career vanishing under the responsibility of sponsoring a madman into these august circles. He manfully had his heart attack poker-faced.

The Head Banker, it seemed, adapting smoothly to my near-exit, had been Reflecting upon the wisdom and virtue of my campaign and found both present in acceptable quantities. This immediately made all the other bankers scramble to jump on my sudden bandwagon and a number of "Well dones" and "Beautifully tailored for today's markets" were heard. One man managed to mention "positioning" and "psychographics" in the first phrase of a single sentence and I stared at him in admiration.

You had to hand it to the Head Banker. He indicated his approval, pressed my hand dryly, and vanished. Which left all the other bankers with an approval from on high and not much knowledge of how to proceed. Tuckerman tried to take over with a few cautious criticisms and improvements but I stopped that by suggesting that we call back the Head Banker and get *his* opinion of such changes.

"Get ready for some heavy-duty billing," I said to Tammy when I got back to the office, and she was happy for me, although it did not appear that she understood what a coup I had just pulled off. One of the problems of being a one-man band is that there's nobody to applaud your triumphs.

Damnit, it *was* a good campaign, even if they did accept it.

Margrit was frying chicken, a quick way to my heart, when I got home. Rather an improvement over Margrit-among-the-missing and she had even brought the chicken. She was wearing one of my button-down shirts, soft cotton to bare legs, that I had abandoned because it was too tight around the middle, cloth shrinkage no doubt. On her, it threatened to wreck the dinner, as I couldn't help investigating what she wore beneath it. She parried my attempts mostly, although I was ready to forgive and forget, softened by the chicken and the shirt and the sheer fact that somebody was doing something nice for me. She had not explained her absence.

Dinner done, she let me repair the kitchen wreckage and curled up on the couch, TV down low enough to be annoying, and announced she needed to talk business.

"Yours or mine?" I asked.

"Both of ours."

"Okay. Whatcha got?" I said, idly playing with shirttail.

"I've got a chance to make some money and I need your help."

"Need a recommendation, want me to call somebody?"

"I need understanding."

The last time Margrit had needed understanding was in a matter of drunkenness at one of my infrequent agency parties which led to her vanishing with a wiseass photographer I particularly detested. The photographer got no more work from me, but insisted on dropping in now and again with a smirk.

Edfelter said I was being paranoid about the smirk and was not amused when I retorted, "The paranoid is often right."

"What's to understand?" I said, all defenses coming up.

"I'm going to do a movie."

I looked at her on the couch, curled and sweet and barely a trace of lines around the corners of her eyes, vulnerable of course and not acknowledging it. I had a rush of empathy about the way she lived and what she had to fight with and how tough it was, eroding everything of value by taking the easy way out, the casting office couch revisited, and time closing down the options. It made me cold inside. We joked about whoring in the agency business but the real thing was much too brutal for me. Perhaps Margrit was made of sterner stuff. I loved her for a moment then, loved her and wanted to protect her, sure that whoever she was dealing with—a movie for god's sake—was just as bad as me and nowhere near as soft or kind.

"A movie?"

"Don't start that," she snapped, and went to the kitchen and I heard the clink of bottles.

"Okay," I yelled, "tell me about the movie."

"Well," she said, coming back to the couch with drink, none for me, "it's not a real movie-movie."

"Jane Fonda doesn't have to worry yet?"

She missed the joke and explained she was to model bathing suits and "maybe some topless stuff" and the money was good and she felt that taking money from me was destroying her feelings toward me because she resented it.

"You've done all that before," I said. "What's the problem?" I was cold-scared in the belly.

"Well, this is a little different, it's videotape."

I waggled my hand what difference.

She was quiet for a moment, fascinated with her drink and the TV, and I waited. "It might be a bit more," she said, "I'm not sure." Long pause. "And we're going to Mexico to shoot it."

"Who's we?" I said, struggling with my face.

"Rod." Rod was the smirky photographer of course and for one manic instant I thought the whole reason he was doing this, defrauding Margrit with promises of porn stardom, was to get me. I started to tell her so and realized that was hardly flattering and started to think of sixty rational reasons why this was a bad idea and got all tangled up and said nothing. She took my silence as an accusation, which it was.

"Look," she said angrily, "I've got to get it where I can and things haven't been all that wonderful and I like Rod even if you don't."

"I seldom like people who fuck my girlfriend!"

We were coiling now, separating instinctively, facial muscles tight and hands clawed, voices overcontrolled. Aggression stimuli, bodily reactions, mind racing, wanting to place the darts just *so*, no room for error, defensive tensing, all this and probably the total movement involved was an inch or so.

"You fool," she said, and her voice was acid and ice. "Men have been wanting to fuck me since I was thirteen, why should Rod be any different?"

"And most of them succeeded," I said bitterly, and she slapped the shit out of me.

"So what," she hissed. "So fucking what. Want to hear about them? You know how *that* turns you on. Want the nasty little details, creep?"

"I'm not a creep when you need money," I said. "Not when the rent's due. Not when you want something."

And, predictably, she started crying, all she wanted was to be normal, house and home, children, all that stuff, and she believed what she was saying at the moment, girl-child dreams broken on the street, so forth. Have to make money, other woman do it, what's so bad about it, what's the difference, might be a big chance, she was sorry she said that, wasn't true.

She looked good crying and I wondered for a crazy moment if a movie career might be a real possibility before reality came flooding in.

"Okay, okay," I said, comforting and getting aroused as she pressed against me crying. "Okay! Do what you have to do, but *think* about it, will you? If Rod's doing a fuck movie, the creep, think before you get involved because once he's got the film, there's not a damn thing you can do about it."

"It's videotape," she said tearfully.

We went to bed and she was wonderful, magnificent, beyond belief, everybody's sex is different and there's no real way to describe it but she transcended everything we'd ever had and even that was right up there.

What kind of guy gets involved with a girl who makes dirty movies? I was having a hard time separating egos and consciences and stuff. I had set the rules, no strings, we're all adults here, and I felt like crying like a child, bullies took my best things away and I didn't protect them like a man. Besides, I liked nasty movies, a middle-aged syndrome if there ever was one.

In the morning she was asleep when I left and in the afternoon the phone rang nine times at my house with no answer.

Maybe I should reconsider the strings. Too late.

5

T UCKERMAN WAS PISSED WITH NO
real good way to relieve it and he chose to be petty-
shitty in hopes of balming his ego. Or something. I didn't
know and was piss-y enough to challenge him. We were
in his middle-rank office, Formica instead of rosewood,
fighting over production art boards, the materials ready
for various printers and engravers, and he found fault
with the placement of commas and the typeface we used
and probably even the flapping paper that protected the
art board.

I dropped his boss on him a couple of times, referring
back to my triumphant meeting, and that did nothing to
make him feel better. By the time a half hour of this had
passed neither one of us could see what we were looking
at because we were too busy trying for an edge.

I was conscious of a feeling of regret and contrasted his behavior to some of my industrial clients of the past, now mostly in Chapter Eleven thanks to the oil slump/crash, and how they would get enthused about a campaign or an ad and how they'd haul in the secretaries to glory in the artwork and how *nice* it could be to do this kind of work when the work was the desired end result. When it became horn-butting or ego measuring, it was no fun at all, probably nothing is, but I was damned if he was going to win.

Margrit was probably on an airplane heading south. Chartered.

Tuckerman finally got through picking and carping and took away the artwork, to show it to the higher-ups.

"Can't you just approve it, Tom?" I asked innocently.

He didn't bother to reply but left quickly before I could accompany him. I didn't feel like chasing him down the hall, so I sat. And sat. All his papers were encased in folders and I started going through the nearest one, ear cocked for his return, although how I expected to hear him in that tomb was problematical at best. Banker stuff. What I was doing was tacky and I knew it. Did it anyhow.

The second folder was more banking, a list of deposits, big money, frequent entries. The company name was vaguely familiar, American Title Investment Group Limited, Inc. I once worked for an advertising agency with five names and the owners insisted that the receptionist use all five when she answered the phone. "Lebest, Cunningham, Walsh, Victor, and Charney." We went through a lot of receptionists and I maintained the name was the problem. Had *my* name been on the door, I might have seen it differently.

I put the folder down and walked out to the door. Tuckerman's secretary smiled at me, sympathetically I thought. Her hair was a strange variant of red.

"How long?" I said.

"I'm sorry, Mr. Beaumont, he's in Mr. Bechman's office."

I shrugged and went back to wait. If I knew Tuckerman, he'd go get a cup of coffee just to be one up. I remembered where I'd seen that name. American Title Investment Group Limited, Inc., was neither American nor had anything to do with titles, if memory served. Instead, it had been an object of frustration to two successive grand juries and the TV cameras had caught the nominal owners after days of testimony looking remarkably like movie gangsters as they hustled to their big black cars, muttering, "No comment," at a great rate. Not nice people. Cocaine, protection rackets, unlicensed pilots, missing witnesses, a confusing legal tangle of overlapping ownership of dummy companies, the works. Not nice at all. Concrete overcoats custom-made from plush executive offices.

I wondered what this bank was doing with them and went back to the folder with more interest. I took it to the couch, a love seat size only for Tuckerman's rank, and was trying to decipher the bankerese when the door opened.

"Would you like some coffee while you wait?" she asked.

With a move that any NFL wide receiver might envy, I turned my straightening up into a stretch and yawned before I answered in the negative. Never saw me dump the damning folder. But she paused to scan the office before she retreated and closed the door. The folder and all its contents were now in the portfolio case which had carried my artwork. I sat down and busied myself with the stuff in it, including a new copy of *Car and Driver* and a three-hundred-dollar check which we had somehow not deposited immediately. As I suspected, the door opened again and she bustled in to straighten up the desk, watching me suspiciously all the while. After she left, I immediately retrieved the folder and put it back on Tuckerman's desk and none too soon since Himself came back and grudgingly gave me the artwork.

"Everybody loves it?" I said.

"You may go ahead."

"But do they love it," I asked, just to be nasty.

"It's approved, go ahead," he said, and picked up one of his folders. Poor sport. As I was leaving, his secretary was poised to enter the office and her good-bye was curt.

I didn't care and I didn't care about Tuckerman's surliness, I had an approved campaign and an approved campaign is like free whiskey for a drunk. I went back to the office, kissed Tammy on the end of her rather attractive nose, and started calling for the suppliers to pick up the stuff. What did you do last week, Beaumont? Oh, I invented the motorcycle and revolutionized bank advertising.

When all of the stuff was out and Tammy had said good-night, I called my house and Margrit's apartment and nobody was home at either place, first time I had called since movie announcement night, willpower or pride working hard. I assumed this meant Margrit really was going to do it, whatever the movie turned out to be, and that was a crusher, four days out on a foul video voyage. Should I have proposed?

I went from a completed-campaign high to naked nasty fear, giant sick visions flashing in my brain, shaky hands, fumbling, and violent indigestion in a moment. I couldn't believe I had repressed all this stuff for all the time I was selling to Tuckerman and I wanted to call Edfelter or my mom. Instead I mixed another drink and sat there and watched the sky and when the sun came in the window and got in my eyes I let it. I must have called her apartment fifty times.

I spent the night on the couch, with Bullit for company, and I remember very little of what I did, although I knew

I couldn't drive. Bullit ate Viennas from the can and burped.

Goddamnit, she couldn't act a lick.

I made some jokes about it too, twisting the words
while slurping down the booze, a truly tragic figure or
something. I didn't like any of the Beaumonts my mind
could conjure up and I was glad when the fog settled in so
I couldn't see myself being so stupid.

I WOKE UP WITH A CUP OF COFFEE
under my nose and a fuzzy vision of blond spikes wavering in the background. I blinked a couple of times and the
vision became Tammy, who was trying her best to appear
as if I slept on the couch as a matter of course.

"Good morning," I said unoriginally, spilling coffee.

"You spent the night," she said.

"Yeah. In my own irrepressible, madcap fashion." I
sipped at the coffee, which had too much Sweet 'n Low in
it, and wondered what I had done in the wee hours.
There were no signs of physical damage, the car keys were
in my pocket, and Bullit was wagging her tail with her
usual enthusiasm. I drank coffee.

Tammy had wisely left and I tottered to the john, feeling the abuse I had put myself through. I didn't throw up for PR reasons. Might as well leave her an illusion or two. Outside I could hear her telling somebody I was in a meeting and I was, I was meeting my future and finding it untoward.

One hangover is not like another and I was a world-class expert on the differences. This one was well within tolerances and I decided that Tammy had to know at some time, so I finished the coffee and went to the kitchen and got an icy-cold beer and gagged it down. I know they say it isn't helpful, but empirical evidence showed "them" to be wrong. I felt much better once the beer decided to stay down. I wondered if this could be the basis for a beer campaign, "Best for the morning after," and decided that my advertising judgments were weak this morning.

"Whatever it is, it can wait," I said on my way out, and headed home. There was a note tucked into my burglar bars, which I had reinforced, replacing the original screws with four-inch number twelve flathead wood screws. If burglars wanted to kick down *my* bars they had best be prepared to take the whole door frame down with them. Maybe that's why they picked on the neighbors.

"Must see you!!!" wrote Tuckerman. I didn't even know he knew where I lived. I crumpled the note and stuck it in my pocket and headed for stage two of the restoration process, a long, hot sudsy shower. Thank God for a good water heater.

I got back in time for lunch and had nobody to eat with. Tammy was gone and had left a stack of phone messages. Three were from Tuckerman, in increasing degrees of urgency. I suspected my newfound billings were about to be abandoned as they had probably discovered forty million in bad energy loans or some such. He was at lunch but I called anyway and wonder of wonders he answered his own phone.

"Beaumont!" he said. "You've got to get it back to me, this afternoon. Now!"

"What are you talking about?" I said.

"Goddamn you," he shouted. "You don't know what you're fooling with! They'll blame me. If they find out . . ."

"Tom," I said. "Speak slowly. Calm down. What the shit are you talking about?"

"You were in my office and you went through my desk, I'll get you for this!"

"What," I said dumbly, flashing back.

"Beaumont," he said, and I could feel him fighting for control. "You were in my office yesterday. I went to show the art to Mr. Bechman. Thelma says you were fooling with my desk. Now the file is missing, a paper from the folder, I've got to have it back immediately! Now!" He was screaming quietly.

"I thumbed through some old files when you made me wait."

"You took a reconciliation and recap sheet from the ATIG file folder!"

"I didn't take a damn thing from your desk," I said. "I don't want anything from your desk! You're nuts. Does Mr. Bechman know how you're treating the people, professionals, who work for you?" ATIG was American Title Investment Group but I had to write it out on a piece of scratch paper to be sure. I wasn't proud of "professionals" but what was I? A vendor?

"If you speak to Bechman . . ." The man was virtually strangling on the other end of the line and I looked at the receiver in amazement. Most unbankerly.

"Tom," I asked, "have you been snorting during work?"

"Bring it back! Now!" And he slammed down the phone. The guy was nuts. I felt trapped and guilty, fingers firmly in the pie. But I hadn't taken his dumb file. I remembered how I had stowed it in the portfolio and went to check.

Whoops. The sheet of paper I had scanned in his office was in fact in the portfolio, stuck against a piece of tape which held flapping paper and which had rolled back so the sticky side was up. The little shit was absolutely right. I took it out, checked the portfolio to see if any more pieces had come home with me, and went directly to the Xerox. If Tuckerman was *that* upset, I'd better have a copy. Then I went back to see what I had. The Xerox didn't reproduce the blue part of the bank's logotype, I thought that careless of the designer.

I am no banker but the pattern was clear, a record of deposits made to three accounts, which were trading money back and forth. In a separate column, deposits into American Title Investment Group's account. I could not see a pattern until I took a total of the original deposits from the left column and ran a tape. Then I compared that to the total deposits into ATIG's account. The two matched perfectly, I wish my company checkbook was that balanced.

What I didn't understand is why it was so obvious. If I could figure it out, it wasn't really hidden, so why the big deal?

There was a coded key by each original deposit and I could find no correlations. If these were separate banks, even in separate cities, and the transactions covered by faked invoices and processed through three sets of books, there would be nothing to link them. I was beginning to understand why Tuckerman was upset. They'd have to keep some sort of record, just to know how much money they had there amid the created confusion, and my sheet of paper apparently was it. A ledger for what my grandfather would have called "monkey business." My grandfather wouldn't read other people's files. Poor Tuckerman.

I decided to let him sweat it, I owed him something.

Then I decided I was crazy and I'd better figure out a way to get this sheet of paper back to him, without saying anything about the Xerox. He had a leather-bound blotter on the desk, could I somehow slip it underneath that? Go visit him, get him out of the office somehow, and slip it under his desk. Stash it in Thelma's area, the orange rat fink?

I went through half a dozen scenarios and finally decided to go downtown in the morning and simply drop the offending paper in the hall somewhere, preferably near Tuckerman's office. If they found it before the cleaning people tossed it, it was their error or Tuckerman's. If they didn't find it, same difference.

It seemed like a good idea at the time.

FROM THE VERY BEGINNING, IT WAS
obvious I would make a very poor CIA agent. I felt guilty.
Guilt leaped from my pores and must have been blind-
ingly apparent to the most casual passerby. A pretty girl at
the elevator greeted me with a "Good afternoon" and I
shrank from her. When I got to Tuckerman's office, I had
not allowed for the receptionist, not Tuckerman's snoopy
secretary, but the overall receptionist. I couldn't figure out
how to get past her and in the process of casually loitering
in the hallway I saw not one, but two bankers who had
been in the advertising meeting.

I decided that subterfuge was not my style and barged
into Tuckerman's office.

"Is this what you're looking for?" I waved the offending paper in front of him and he came across the desk like
a rocket and snatched it away.

"Goddamnit, Beaumont, you have no business . . . you shouldn't touch . . . goddamnit!" Tuckerman was not my friend and he glared at me, red-faced, unable to summon up a threat or a punishment sufficiently severe. He generated an impressive amount of anger.

"It fell into the portfolio," I said lamely.

"Just jumped off my desk, right?"

"No," I said. "I was looking for something to read while I was waiting—you did make me wait, remember?—and I picked up the nearest file."

He glared at me and I met his eyes with some difficulty. I didn't have any business going through his stuff, what can I say? I was wrong. Unfortunately, I got caught, which seems to happen to me a lot. I mentally vowed to aim closer to the straight and narrow. Tuckerman got up and closed his door.

"Look," he said. "This must stay between us. If they found out you had even seen this . . ."

"Who's they?" I asked.

"Don't worry about it. Just keep quiet. I can handle Thelma and just you keep quiet. You really can't imagine how important that is." He drifted away, anger gone as quickly as it came, probably thinking of what to do with Thelma. He came back to the present with a jerk.

"You haven't shown this to anyone? Did you read it?"

"I glanced at it. Bunch of deposits or something," I said.

"It's just an internal document," he said. "Not very interesting, eh?" His laugh was worse than my imitation of a spy and I joined him. Thelma stuck her head in the door and informed him that Mr. Bechman wanted him on the double and he blanched and stuffed the offending piece of paper in his desk and locked the drawer. He was hurrying down the hall before I could get out of the office and I looked at Thelma. She had a righteous simper plastered all over her narrow, foxlike face and I decided her hair looked like orange-red plastic. I had never paid a whole lot of attention to Thelma. I wondered what kind of a shit would have people around who whitened when summoned to his office. Thelma was probably a star in Bechman's book for informing on her boss. Maybe it was jealousy, I thought. At my office everybody took things off my desk and didn't return them.

"I mentioned to Mr. Bechman about your going through Mr. Tuckerman's desk and the missing paper," she said.

"Good!" I said. "Good work! We will make sure your alertness is rewarded." And I made a point of shaking her hand. It was just a touch clammy. Excitement, probably. Thelma got her rocks off reporting all the nasty things the other little girls did, I suspect. I sketched a salute when I left.

I stopped by the world's best tackle shop on the way back and spent an hour and a half deciding whether I needed, really needed, another popping rod. I already had about a dozen, hung around the walls of the bayhouse, but you can never have too many fishing rods and I charged them so it wasn't like real money. I treated myself to a splendid solitary lunch to boot. Going back to the office, I listened to talk radio so I could shout comments and criticisms to it, Bullit wagging agreement from her perch on the rear deck.

The periodic helicopter traffic report was a shocker: "Avoid the intersection of Smith and Caroline because Emergency Services has the right two lanes blocked off following the fatal accident. Alternate routes are . . ." I had just been there, looking down from Tuckerman's office.

The regular newscaster came in on top with more details. "This just in. Tom Tuckerman, a local banking executive, fell to his death from the thirty-fourth floor of the Americana Tower in downtown Houston. Details are sketchy but apparently Tuckerman was in the penthouse suite of the bank, which serves as their executive of-fices . . .''

I wondered if Thelma was pleased. It *had* to be an acci-dent. What the dickens they were doing out in the pent-house garden, I couldn't say. But it had to be an accident. I wished I hadn't given him such a hard time.

A sharp reprimand should have done it. Maybe the bank had been hanging around American Title too much.

I drove on autopilot while my mind skittered. My expe-rience with people dying was odd. You don't know people who die. Although when I worked for a large agency and wore suits daily, I had three women working for me. For Christmas I gave them each a tiny, hand-carved Indian pin, a ladybug for the traffic manager who stayed on my back, a warrior for the designer who fought me con-tinually, and a hatchet for the pasteup girl. Over the years, two of the ladies had lost their pins and both were now dead, one in a freak traffic accident and one of mysterious causes in Italy. The other person, who was one of my dearest friends, guarded hers like it was gold. I had diffi-culty remembering what the other two looked like, my mind pushing away the thought of death. My grand-mother looked like a painting-on-velvet in her coffin and I knew it wasn't her.

Tuckerman was too close and too vivid. Probably one of those freaky accidents.

What about the campaign? He had shown it to Bech-man. It was ''approved.'' Should I proceed and pretend it never happened? I was hung up on the protocol and prac-ticality of his death and, honestly, not too terribly sad-dened. I wonder who they'd give me to work with?

Just a freaky accident.

Tammy had the radio blasting when I walked in the back door. Her blonde spikes bounced as she bent to turn it down and I couldn't help but notice that she came equipped with an outstanding chest. I was saved from

being a dirty old man by noticing and being generally un-
moved. She stayed bent a fraction too long and I looked
again. Outstanding.

"Some man is calling for you but hanging up," she
said.

"How do you know it's for me?"

"He calls and asks for you and when I say you're out he
hangs up right away. He's called twice."

"Well I'll be here next time."

"*I* won't. I have an appointment and I'll bet you'll let
me off early," she said.

"Why?" I asked.

"Because I let you get a free peek." She grinned and
picked up her purse. I told her about Tuckerman and she
was shocked. Asked me if we were still doing the campaign, in brutal selfishness. Equally selfish, I nodded and
she left, floating a cliché behind her.

She normally put the phone over to the answering service but I waved her to forget it while I was trying to
think up a snappy rejoinder. They have you cold, at any
age, no matter how smooth you try to be.

The phone was not ringing much which meant that we
must be fairly well paid up and I had an answer for most
of the questions asked in the next hour. I was upstairs,
rummaging through the art files, when the first after-five
call came in. I had meant to forward the phone.

"Beaumont?"

"Yes."

"Stay there." And he hung up. It must have been
Tammy's caller and he had an unpleasant voice. "Fuck
you," I said to the dead phone, and went back to my
search. I finally found the production flat I was looking
for and went downstairs.

He was square. A couple inches shorter than I and a
foot broader. He looked neckless and the turtleneck
sweater, black, of course, was not meant for Houston's

climate in mid-April. I smiled anyway and offered my hand which was a mistake because he deliberately tried to crush my knuckles, staring straight into my face as he did. I was uneasy at first sight and verging on scared after his first sentence. He was why doors have dead bolts. Only an idiot wouldn't have locked up after the phone call.

"You're supposed to advertise, not snoop," he stated.

"Excuse me, I missed your name."

"I didn't give it," he said, staring.

"Well, what can I do for you?" I said, edging my body around Tammy's desk.

"Nice office." He walked past me into the middle office, now unoccupied, where the magazines were and the supply closet and the Xerox.

"Got your own Xerox and everything," he said to himself. "Makes a whole bunch of copies."

"Are you selling copiers?" I asked from the doorway.

"I'm selling peace of mind," he said without looking at me. "Peace of mind is what you get when you don't snoop. Or, make copies of things that don't belong to you."

Unfortunately, my voice cracked when I told him to get out and he grinned. Then he walked over to the neat desk, picked up the Selectric from the return, cord ripping loose from the wall, and walked over and smashed it into the Xerox. Glass splattered.

I did the first smart thing since he arrived and bolted out the front door. I could hear Bullit in full cry behind me, roused from her sleeping couch by the destruction. When I dared to look back, he was standing in the doorway of my office and I swear he was smiling. I zipped around the corner and made for the nearest phone, which was at the Circle K down the block. The Vietnamese guy watched in amazement from his perch as I pounded down the street. More legends for you, buddy.

Where was Bullit? I looked over my shoulder and the

bitch was prancing around, tail all fluffy, in front of a pair of slavering Dobermans who were behind a fence and not liking it. She wasn't even in heat.

I yelled and yelled louder and she rewarded me with a glance and then got into an idiotic game of race-up-'n-down-the-fence. She was precious and adorable, just ask her.

I could see my assailant or actually the office's assailant getting into a Buick and grinning at my plight and I was overcome with a red anger which almost made me go back and beat the shit out of him. Almost, because I felt it an impossible task, not destined to happen, and I cursed my age and my fears and even the frustration that kept me from leaving the damn dog and calling the cops, and just once I'd like to get the macho things right, despite all the antimacho sentiment everybody has, it's not a bad thing actually. It's what I thought I should be and I disappointed myself again.

I was almost crying when I got to the phone. Bullit came prancing up and I had no place to tie her so I picked her up and held her under my arm when I discovered I didn't have a quarter for the call.

F~OR A PEACE-LOVING, COWARDLY,~
and generally law-abiding citizen (the grass stash hardly
counted these days), I certainly saw the police on a frequent basis. The radio car that came to the office con-
tained a paunchy sergeant who had seen everything at
least twice and didn't much care. A little Xerox damage by
an unknown perp didn't faze him a bit.

"Maybe I could write it up as breaking and copying,"
he said with a straight face, waiting to see if I got the joke
before laughing a two-bark laugh.

Yes, I owned the building and the Xerox, no, I didn't
recognize the man, no, I wasn't in hock or having family
difficulties, yes, I owed people but they weren't the sort to
send over a hardguy, no, I wasn't involved with cocaine
("nose-candy," winked Sergeant Dole), yes, I wanted to
press charges.

He stayed long enough to send his rookie partner, new-ness glistening from hat brim to polished steel-toed shoes, out to the car so he could do away with about four ounces of my bourbon, refusing scotch as "too high-class" and I agreed silently. He inspected my door locks as he left and entered the car shaking his head.

I saw that both of them were laughing like mad when they drove away.

I called Tammy and apparently interrupted something, which was a bit of a shock and I don't know why because she's certainly old enough. When we got over our shared embarrassment, I told her to take a vacation.

"Why?" she asked, and I was stumped for a second.

"Because we're having some trouble I don't want you involved in," I said. It took some argument, but she agreed to take a week and call me at home before coming back. Bullit thought the office mess very interesting and sniffed it out, piece by piece. The phone rang and it was Margrit, on a bad connection from Cabo San Lucas, charges reversed. That's Baja, not Mexico, I thought, try-ing to deal with the operator.

How are you, everything's fine, the movie is more than I expected but going well, interesting, beautiful water, you'd love to fish it, everything's okay. Glass tinkling. Not sure when she'd be back, peasants unfriendly, behave my-self, would I stave off HL&P for her, bill at my house, Rod says hello.

Then I had to clean up, tears welling. That's one thing you don't see on the ten o'clock news, the mess, the sheer physical mess involved in our aberrations. I'd hate to see the scene of a murder. Tuckerman's dead, what about the funeral. The cleanup finished the bourbon, shared with Sergeant Dole, but I was determined to go home whiskey breath and all.

I wonder if there was something wrong with my locks, speaking of Sergeant Dole.

I wonder if Rod was better than me?

I drove rather well, considering the whiskey, and parked the 'Vette three blocks off and before I got home I was frightened. I improvised a lead for Bullit and went in the back way, climbing through a gap in the cedar fence I should have fixed long ago. I didn't turn on a light, feeling my way through the familiar house, and fell over the TV set. Bullit was growling deep in her throat and as my eyes adjusted, irising down, I saw another mess, this one considerably worse and I was afraid to turn on a light.

TV set on its side on the floor, books slipping under my feet, kitchen cabinets thrown open, bedrooms much the same, what were they doing to me? I stealthily peered through every curtain, looking for watchers, and saw an empty street, neighbor's cars identifiable, lights glowing in windows, where were they?

How did I know to be frightened before I got home?

I didn't have the answer and I was too scared to be mad, self-preservation taking precedence, the impudent casualness of these felonies as frightening as anything.

Out again, Bullit confused, back down the dark street, trying to slump my height, into the car and away. I went directly to the Pulse machine and got out as much cash as it would give me, two hundred plus another sixty or so in the pocket, and went to the wrong side of town.

Houston has several wrong sides, depending in part on your ethnic persuasion. What I considered frightening was home to little girls with black or brown faces. I went to the Eastex freeway, used car lots lining the road, interrupted by Mr. Chicken, Circle K, PAWN, *Se Habla Español*, lots of explanation points, came four to the sign kit no doubt. Stashed the noticeable car at Houston Intercontinental, grabbed a cab, and headed for a motel. There was a constant roar of freeway traffic, yellow flashing portable signs, arrows, and I paid for one night cash, nineteen bucks, for a hot-sheet room and a suspicious black face craned at the cab, where's the girl?

I didn't think Sergeant Dole would approve but I doubted he wanted to baby-sit me and I didn't want to take six-two of trouble near any of my friends, so the nineteen bucks seemed like a bargain, although I could hear angry voices raised now and then that made me doubt the smartness of this move. I wanted to disappear inside this seedy room, at least until the all-clear sounded. That could take days, I supposed, while trying to go to sleep.

The hardest part of it was not being able to use my credit cards. Ah, credit cards. At one point in my life I had viewed them as a symbol of maturity, a big-people badge. Then at another, sadder time I tore them all up discovering that the manufacturers had created some very tough plastics. Now my attitude had moderated—toward credit cards and much else—and they were a convenient part of my normal life.

I carried a Gold American Express for my personal business as opposed to my business-business. I carried Exxon and Texaco and Firestone for the car, MasterCard, the Pulse card, which got me cash from the bank, a card for the Y, and a couple of others, one expired. Almost anything a man could want was chargeable, maybe including the free-lance services of one of the ladies at my friend Vince's place, the Foxy Lady. As my libido was at an all-time low, I didn't need that but perhaps Vince could be useful, I thought he knew the protocols and manners of this frightening world.

I couldn't use the cards because I was convinced they left a trail, a mysterious computer trail that whoever was fucking up my life could use. The image of the TV on the floor in my blacked-out house kept coming back. It was "they" again, the mysterious all-powerful "they" we talk about. They were behind all this, surely. I was beginning to revise my thinking about poor Tuckerman, a victim of "their" power. I was flat scared of "them," faceless as they were. They could trace me, of that I was quite certain, computer access, electronic trails, green words glowing on the screens.

Being chased was nowhere near as exciting as it appeared in the books. I couldn't go to my tattered house and I was afraid to visit the office, although I called the answering service once and was inundated by messages. The agency was careening along like a riderless bike and destined to hit a very substantial tree at any minute. Who's to say "they" can't affect our lives?

The dingy motel was even more dingy by the early morning sun and I was up before the sun both of the days I'd been in residence. The car was at the airport parking lot, a six-buck cab ride away. The toilet would threaten to overflow every time I used it. I stared nervously into the bowl as the water rose higher on every flush, touching the underside of the rim and then reluctantly gurgling out. For this I paid my nineteen bucks and everybody was totally indifferent, from the traffic roaring endlessly on the freeway to the bored maid whom I offended by asking for clean sheets.

I checked out and took a cab to get the car, investing more of my limited funds in outrageous parking fees. I badly needed clothes, I had to find out what was going on, and I needed a phone. A clean Ramada on the Southwest Freeway seemed like a serious step up in my life, although the desk clerk hesitated over accepting my cash, three crisp twenties from the Pulse machine, what did he want. A drugstore visit for a fresh pack of razor blades and toothpaste, a discount store for shorts and a stiff new pair of jeans, and I was set.

Clients first or enemies?

I arranged things carefully, there at the Ramada with hard plastic the overriding motif, Tab can opened, ashtray at hand, notepad and ballpoint from the drugstore ready. I called the bank and hung up when they answered the first time.

The answering service was exasperated with me, no notice when you're out of town, what are we to say, where is Tammy, and the client calls were staggering, enough so that I was more impressed with my business than before. I folded the sheet with the list of numbers on it and called downtown again.

This time I hung on to my courage and didn't hang up and my voice sounded good and firm when I jousted with Mr. Bechman's secretary.

"Tell him Beaumont's on the line and see," I suggested after she told me he was not taking calls. She could have said in a meeting but Bechman was sufficiently important that his secretary told the truth. His voice was just as cold as his eyes and I wondered what he was like when he made love to his wife with those perfect hands.

"Please be quick, Mr. Beaumont, I have an overseas call holding," he said. Maybe it was true.

"What are you doing to me?"

"Please be specific."

"Tuckerman's dead, a thug smashed up my office, my house was ransacked, and I've been hiding for two days, is that specific?"

"I have no knowledge of any of this," he said, and hung up.

I looked at the phone like it was a snake. I wondered could he trace it, if he wanted to trace it, wouldn't he have kept me on the line, why did he hang up, did this mean he wouldn't be a client anymore, if he really had nothing to do with all of this, I had well and truly fucked up. "They" would add it to my tab.

I checked out and went to my office and I hadn't been there thirty minutes when they showed up. I kicked over the chair and went out the back, straight into the arms of No-Neck's small friend, who managed to get me back behind my desk without much effort. What he had done with my hand was painful and I wanted to bend over it and cry but they wouldn't let me.

"Now," said No-Neck, "let's have a nice talk."

9

SOMEHOW IT WAS WORSE BECAUSE IT was in my office. Over the years I had become accustomed to calling the two-story house mine and feeling like here was a place where I was king, or at least the clown prince. I made decisions, affected people, made things happen. Now I was in my chair, slammed there by No-Neck, and very much not in control. Being in my office galled my already tattered pride.

Habits are a wonderful way to ease through the day without being burdened by a billion tiny decisions. However, you'd think I would have been smart enough to lock up the office, given my circumstance. Habit. Even my thoughts fell into a routine these days, repetitive concepts floating up to the forebrain from routine stimulus, I always started my shower by washing my left forearm too. Why didn't I lock the bloody doors?

You get so far away from the physical, the sheer domi-
nation of muscle and brawn and willingness to use both.
When was I last physically confronted? Eighth grade, I
think, a dispute over budding sexual favors, brick wall
grinding at my back, serious teenage faces glaring, terror
making me mute. It was all so long ago. And I remember
poor performance grades even then, in the unforgiving
male scorecard we all carry.

I started to protest and bluster but cut myself off short
when they exchanged grins and I settled for a simple
question, glad my voice was under control.

"What can I do for you, gentlemen?" Plenty of spin on
the "gentlemen" and they grinned more.

"Let's talk about paper," the other one said. He was a
little guy, weight lifter, I suspect, given to shirts that fitted
tightly around bulging biceps, tight-tight jeans, no belt,
balanced obviously on his feet. He was probably hell in
the bars.

"Carnival Craft, Hammermill Bond, Currency Cover?"

"Paper that your little snoopy nose shouldn't have
snooped on." He flicked an indifferent hand at my nose
and I ducked back so he missed, which upset my balance
a bit in the executive chair and I caught the edge of the
desk to keep upright.

"You assholes," I said. The blow came from No-Neck
and I never saw it. My head rang and my ear burned
where his open hand had smashed it and I knocked a
sheath of paper, media reports, off the desk with my face.
I felt tiny.

"You're still assholes," I said out of some stupid pride,
and I lost a few seconds tangled up with the chair on the
floor, hurting now on the temple, sticky wetness dripping
from the eyebrow, head buzzing so that I had to crane to
hear.

"Pay attention and attempt to be nice," said the small
one.

"What?"

"Pay attention. We know you were in some files you shouldn't have been in. It was extraordinarily sloppy." He extended his hand to help me up, repeating "sloppy."

"It has been corrected," he said.

Tuckerman. Told them all about my tacky snooping, doubtless, who would not? Watch the first step, Tom, it's a biggie. Tuckerman or his plastic-hair secretary. I wondered if she had been "corrected" too.

"Let's cut all this shit," I said, and they both nodded politely. "I can't think of any paper like you're talking about except some files I saw while I was waiting for Tom. Tuckerman, Tom Tuckerman. Is that what you're talking about?"

They were pleased. No-Neck motioned me to continue. He didn't seem to be favoring his hand and I thought you were never supposed to hit anybody in the head with your hand. Advertising people didn't count, soft heads.

"So . . . what?" I said.

"Tell us what you saw," said No-Neck, and raised a cautioning hand. "We already know, so don't lie."

"If you already know . . ." I said, and flinched when the small one poised to hit again. "Okay. I saw a file . . ." memory gone blank, any name but American Title Investment Group, had to be a file that was on the desk, I'd bet my life they'd inventoried, maybe I'd lost. Tuckerman knew. I held up a hand, wait, and said, "Some trucking company." Thanks, brain cells. It had been the first file I had scanned what seemed like months ago.

They were not pleased but I went on. "Yeah. A trucking company. Loans on the vehicles, long serial numbers, partial payments for . . . two? . . . months, somebody wrote 'Foreclose' on the cover memo and I was thinking about my own loans."

"Don't worry about your loans," said No-Neck. "What else?"

"I don't know," I said.

"Think exceptionally hard," said the small guy.

"I looked at a couple others. The truck loans were the most interesting, poor sonuvabitches."

"We're burnin' daylight," said No-Neck.

I said, "Tell me what you want to know and I'll tell you. All I want is you out of here." Hearing my voice did nothing for my sense of manliness. I had weaseled out of the encounter years ago and nothing changes. Macho, macho.

"Quite reasonable," said the small one. "We are specifically interested in a file for American Title Investment Group, which should never have been exposed. What did you see in it?"

"Was that there?" I said, and threw up an arm to block No-Neck's swing which got me a sore forearm and my own hand hit me in the eye and it started to water.

"Let's do it and get out," he said.

"I suggest you be prompt," said the smaller thug.

"I may have seen it, so what?" I said through tears.

"What did you see, precisely?"

"I've got the files jumbled in my head," I said. "One had a long list of deposits, was that it?"

"Bingo," said No-Neck.

"Ah yes, a long list of deposits," said the little one. "These were deposits *by* ATIG or *to* them?"

"Frankly," I said, "I don't remember."

And they went to work, contemptuously and casually and I hurt, boiling with rage inside, one good punch on No-Neck, too low, my hand swelling and I was on the floor again with no clear memory of what they had done but I hurt in several places and my breath was gone, oh God, I couldn't catch a breath and I was doubled over, a vacuum in my lungs, and it took several minutes to get back to some semblance of normal.

"Which," said my small friend. "The last asshole we talked to ended up shitting his pants."

I started to pick up some of the stuff from the floor, a crow which some fool had stuffed for me and a racquet-ball trophy from the Y, mixed doubles, and No-Neck sat me down again.

"Deposits to American Whoever," I said. "I think."

"And, of course, you used your handy-dandy Xerox machine to make copies for all the kids," said No-Neck. "Oh, it seems to need repair now! Maybe your kids will too!"

"No," I said, "I didn't use the Xerox."

"Just what did you use?" asked the other.

"I've got a stat camera upstairs," I said.

They looked blank. I said, "I've got a stat camera, a big fixed camera which makes photostats and veloxes. I use it in my work."

"It makes copies?"

"It makes a negative and then you can make enlargements. Or reductions, whatever. You make a print, larger or smaller, from the negative."

"And you have a negative." Small One didn't like this.

"Yes."

"So you could make a great number of prints."

"No, for that you use the Xerox. You use the stat camera to make the original a size you can Xerox. If it's too big or small. Mostly I use it for . . ."

"You made a negative," he interrupted.

"Yes, but I didn't make any prints. I don't know why but I thought I should have a copy, Tom was . . ."

"Tom is not a concern here," he interrupted again.

"Okay. I made a negative."

They looked at each other, shaking heads. Poor Beaumont. I didn't want sympathy and I controlled my bladder with difficulty. We might have been discussing the weather.

"Where is the negative?" The smaller guy had taken over the conversation and No-Neck just kept shaking his head. He didn't have to make a muscle, I was impressed enough.

"Upstairs. I didn't want to leave a Xerox around and I'm the only one who knows how to operate the stat camera. So I thought keeping it in negative form was okay." I was crazy. I wanted them to applaud my security measures.

"The blonde doesn't?" No-Neck asked.

"She can barely handle a typewriter," I said. God, I had to keep poor spiky Tammy out of this. "She has other abilities." They didn't leer with me, sorry, Tammy, but I've got to keep you clear and your reputation is a small price.

"Let's go upstairs and you can show us this stat camera," said the little one. "*And* the negative you made."

I could have broken away and made for the door when we went to the stairs and the little man made a point of having his partner go ahead of me, so only he was between me and the outside. He wanted me to try for it, I could feel his readiness, revenge for a gene that made him five-six, but I had no taste for it and took them upstairs to the stat room. The machine sat in the corner, bulky painted metal box, a bank of six floodlights to a side, red safelights in the ceiling fixture. Sign outside the door: DARK. DO NOT ENTER, and I motioned them to the center of the room.

"I have to turn out the lights, so stand still so you don't spill chemicals on yourself," I said.

"Why do you turn out the lights?" asked the leader.

"Because it's a negative, reversed. You can't read negatives, they're reversed. I can't and I work this machine all the time. It will be dark only for a couple of seconds, till I get the paper out of the box," I said patiently, motioning to the metal rack with paper and chemistry. Brown bottles, official-looking, charts on the wall. "Then we'll use the red lights, the paper doesn't react to red."

They both moved closer and I was glad and I fussed with the machine, consulting a chart, pulled out a thirty-five-millimeter negative and forced it into a holder made for four by fives, measuring distances, and set the switches and flipped out the lights.

"Don't move for a minute," I said , and flipped up both banks of floods, hit the switch, and gave them eighteen hundred watts of harsh white light right in the eyes. Their irises were already closing down, adapting to the dark, so the glare was awful, even through my closed eyelids, and I kicked No-Neck squarely in the balls, feeling softness and shape against my instep, and got in one good shot, best I could do through slitted eyes, against the smaller one's head.

He reacted like a cat but I bowled him over by sheer weight and he was clawing at my leg as we came around the corner and I yanked loose and kicked and caught him squarely with my foot and half-fell down the stairs, why hadn't the fools taken my car keys away, made it out the front door toward the car, hearing shouts behind me, into the 'Vette, and started in a flash and out of there with stink of burned rubber in my nose.

I hoped the circuit breakers would kick out before the stat machine burned itself up.

I was driving very fast and controlled, weaving in and out of traffic on Westheimer—when you want the cops they're never there—anticipating the cars ahead, and I was outside the Loop before I caught my breath and that made my decision for me.

The office was still unlocked and they could ravish the Barcelona chairs for all I cared. I would have felt better if it had been a fair fight and over. Shake hands, have a beer, and forget it. My hands were shaking and I burped noisily.

It would have been cleaner if I could have whipped them physically but somewhere in the last decade they had changed the rules. I cringed thinking about what they might have done to me.

10

I SUSPECT I'M IN THE MARKET FOR A new stat camera, I thought, pulling into the dark and shadowed parking lot at the Foxy Lady. Vince kept it dark to hide the customers' cars and personally escorted his dancers, the ones who weren't engaged for the evening, to their vehicles.

Would-be rapists stayed far away from Vince, who generated an impressive array of competence just walking down the hall, six-hundred-dollar suit and you could see the muscles. Natural muscles, no weight lifting or show-manship there. More than size or blond good looks, it was a quality he generated in your head, the awareness that he'd do what he had to, cross at your own risk and don't expect apologies. I had watched him handle drunks, no bouncer needed at Vince's place, polite and firm and he did something that made the worst of them turn whitely sober without noise, the kind of hurting that devoured shouts and they would leave and if they came again they were gentlemen, too refined to really have fun, but you felt safe there.

We were friends from long ago, high school hero makes it reasonably big and tennis-playing friend still hangs around. I was too light then for the football team he led, not that good a team, but Vince played with a kind of ferocious commitment that left more than one opponent knocked cleanly cold and you remember that. He played square too, in a business that often substituted tawdry sex for service or product. At the Foxy Lady you got a solid drink, good food if you wanted it and the drunks had coffee with Vince until he judged them ready for the road.

I make him sound too good. It was a tough racket and he was tough enough with the girls, making them work, delivering value and at least the semblance of sexual excitement in a dubious business but fair, I heard, and they tended to stay with him until the drifting set in, longer than most places. Pretty girls, from the country mostly, a shade better to talk to, the same overpriced drinks of course, when you bought her a drink, a girl's gotta eat and she gets half the price of her fruit-colored cocktail. Amazing amount of breasts on display, you pick size and shape and nipple configuration.

He was not receiving visitors just now and I waited where there was the most concealment, a Pulse machine twenty on the table to cover my tab if I had to run, minding my own business with an occasional smile for a dancer that I knew, gum popping doesn't really work too well with a body like that, barely covered, shaven pubes, and if she dances like that here how would you ever know if it was real?

"Where's Margrit?" Vince asked, half-lifting me out of my chair and stuffing the bill in my coat pocket. We headed for his office, private stock in a crystal glass, good prints on the walls, outdoor stuff mostly, signed and numbered and spotlighted, a room to relax in, where the roar of the dancing music filtered past hardwood paneling and became a comfortable white noise.

"In Mexico, Baja actually, making a movie." His eyebrows did the talking and I dismissed the subject with a wave, feeling a familiar tightening in my gut, oh God not now, I wanted to cry, never before Vince. "I . . . want to sell you the 'Vette."

"My legs are too long. Why?"

"Your legs are the same length as mine and I need the cash. Tonight. There's about eight or nine owing on it and it's worth maybe two thousand on a quick sale, so could you give me that? Two thousand I mean?"

"Beaumont, what's with you? What's going on?"

"You'll have to get the title later, when I can get to my office, but you can use it till then."

"What's going on?" he asked quietly, and I told him the whole story, looking for approval when I told him about the stat camera blindness I'd caused my thugs and explaining why I didn't know if I dared use the credit cards, only two hundred from the ATM a day and I needed cash.

"Shit," he said after a few minutes.

"That's hardly encouraging."

"Shit," he said.

"Come on, Vince, gimme a break. I need help here."

"Beaumont," he said. "You haven't the faintest idea how much help you need. Or what you're into. I don't know nor want to know. You don't want to mess with those people."

He thought for a couple of minutes. "They're a big business and they have a . . . momentum. You know how the government goes into fifty pages of specs to buy a screwdriver? Overkill? Same difference. They start out to do something and they get rolling and they keep on doing it, even when they don't need to. They're detached, the Corporation wants it done, you know?'' He stopped again. "And let the bodies fall where they may," he said to himself. "What do you plan to do?"

"I need to get out of sight. I'm heading to the bay."

"Beaumont, how's the bay paid for?"

"I pay for it."

"How, what method?"

"You mean how do we physically pay for it? We write a check every month. Mortgage interest and principal."

"You write a check and the check gets cashed and there's a record. It's in the machine."

"Oh shit," I said.

"You won't believe how how much they can get about you, even before they start the depth interviews, the 'credit checks' around your neighborhood, talking to your ex-wives, friends, people you do business with. Just checks is enough."

"Jesus, Vince, we're not talking the CIA here!"

"Better if it was."

"Really? Oh come on!"

"What's real? I don't know. But you sound to me like you're over your head."

"I've *been* over my head. From the start. This is not something I do well, Vince. I don't know how to operate."

"It was a good trick with the stat machine."

"Camera."

"Whatever. Stay put." He vanished in the direction of the girls' dressing room and I waited. Vince's office reflected his own decorating taste. The prints, the few piece of good art, large heavy oak table for a desk, and everything neat as a pin. I started to poke through a stack of papers in a manila folder on his desk and yanked my hand back like it was radioactive.

He came back with a medium sheath of bills, handed it to me, and I wrapped it around my useless credit cards and secured the resulting thick wad with a big rubber band. Beaumont's answer to the expensive money clip. The rubber bands came from the Sunday newspaper. I still didn't know where to start.

"Next," said Vince, "we lose your car."

"How do we that?"

"We report it stolen, of course." And he picked up the phone and did exactly that, being indignant for a bored police dispatcher. When he hung up the phone, he motioned for me to follow him.

Walking down the hall, I couldn't avoid staring into the dressing room. Topless dancers have different standards and watching them wander around in various combinations of no or little clothing was fascinating. I told Vince that and he said yes. We took the car a good distance away, bad streets, and he pulled out some wire and alligator clips and hot-wired it, testing the connections by starting the car, all this after yanking the ignition switch boldly out of the steering column with a strange-looking tool.

"You have unexpected talents," I said.

"Took 'em off of a customer who talked too much."

Vince's walk and mine were matched and we were back inside his office in minutes. He opened a drawer in the credenza behind his desk table and handed me a key.

"Eighty-three Chevy van. Current tags. Drive the limit."

"Who's is it?"

"Don't ask. You've got a day or so before they get to your bay place, I would guess. Start thinking—hard— about how to make peace."

"*Can* I make peace?"

"Beaumont," he said. "Consider the alternative."

He told me where the van was, asked me if I owned a

gun—no—and said he'd ask around about American Title Investment Group because he "thought he knew who they were" and told me to get going.

"You are sober?"

"I had half of one drink. Here, give this to the girl at the table, whose table it was, my waitress." I handed him back a ten. I left and wandered through the dark parking lot until I found the van, fumbled my way into it, and was reassured to find familiar-as-Chevrolet controls. The only difference was I felt like I was driving a stepladder, the thing was that tall. It did have a drink holder on the console between the front seats which covered the engine and I wished I had asked Vince for a roadie.

I was going to miss the Corvette.

11

I FOUND A CIRCLE K OUTSIDE OF Sugar Land, just west of Houston, named for the giant sugar company that used to pay its employees in script good at the company store and had founded a whole town to support its plant. Trainloads of bushy sugarcane in, clean white packets out. Their trucks had stainless-steel tanks which could blind you in the summer's sun. Closest thing Houston had to a mining town and now another bedroom community.

I bought a sack of ice and a small foam chest, some munchies, and a six-pack. I also made a long phone call from an outside phone, swatting the moths and various flying critters which swarmed to the lights. I talked to an old friend of mine in the agency business, more successful than I certainly, with dozens of employees and lots of perks, quotes in the trade magazines. I persuaded him to take over my accounts for the duration. I had to cash in all my markers and give an expurgated version of my current history, punctuated by his editorial comments about my sanity. I couldn't really argue but he took the list of client names and a brief status report over the phone and told me it would cost dinner for the four of us, "whichever broad you're messing with then." Then I hit the road.

Driving along U.S. 59, avoiding the speed trap at Kendleton (famous for losing thousands of dollars in traffic fines which were supposed to go to the state), I tried to plan. Foremost among my goals was to avoid No-Neck and friend and whatever they planned to do to me. Tuckerman had shown me the stakes in this particular game and I had to avoid his fate, although it was tough to think seriously about people wanting to kill me. I wondered if Mr. Bechman had called upon the widow. Probably sent flowers and wrote it off. Maybe the American Title goons had it covered with a section in the company manual. What had they in mind for me?

You fire ad agencies and cuss them and tell horror stories about their stupidity but seldom kill them off.

The guy who could call off the dogs was Bechman. I suspected he'd be a tough sell. What I had was a bit of knowledge, a Xerox copy which could easily be disclaimed and they had plenty of time to cover their tracks. What made it more difficult for them to call a truce was their escalation of hostilities. There is possibly a lesson here for governments.

I was perfectly capable of forgiving/forgetting, especially the latter. I felt no real need to right whatever wrongs were represented by that piece of paper which is very probably unworthy but accurate. I didn't think Bechman would accept my assurances, so I needed a lever. When my ass was completely clear and I could count on some sort of future, I would worry about the morality of it all. I was thinking of him as some sort of employee of American Title rather than a big-time banker and that was probably close to the truth.

You can make as many copies as you want with a Xerox.

One way out would be just to send copies of the paper to the newspapers and the radio stations and the TV newspeople. Let them do the Watergate bit, although I had little faith they could do as thorough a job of it. Would they believe me or Bechman, anyhow? I could *tell* the bank people I had arranged for the transmittal of the paper in the event of an accident to me, but they could probably get the whole thing covered up completely by then. It would be a two-day news story at best and I wanted to live a lot longer than that.

I didn't reach a solution. Bechman was a businessman. All I had to do was demonstrate it was smarter and more profitable for him to let me alone. I didn't know then I had made a basic error in my calculations.

The van drove itself, which was surprising since it still felt like a large packing crate, but I could put my brain on autopilot and let the cruise control have it. Some fancy van, cruise control and power windows and captain's chairs and the whole bit. I thought of Margrit and worried about Tammy. The new U.S. 59 was a lot quicker and Point Lookout, where I had my bayhouse, came up on the road signs before midnight. I would ease into the house without bothering anybody, especially Mr. Evans, my friend and fixer of all the things that go wrong at a bayhouse. His yard butted up to mine and his was neater. I'd leave the van back up the shell road, which should make the bayhouse look unoccupied if I was careful with the lights.

I dumped my half-full beer when I got there and fixed a stout bourbon, lots of ice in the big squat glass, also crystal what the hell, and sat and relaxed for the first time in too

many days. I'd take a shower in the dark and worry tomorrow.

I wondered what Margrit was up to.

My recent troubles kept me from whining and moaning
about her and who she was wrapping her legs around
currently. I had forgotten the damn HL&P bill and the
light company was unforgiving. I couldn't help that now,
phrasing excuses in my head. And I had discovered that
being threatened concentrates the mind wonderfully well.
"Live for the now," I said, thinking of good ole Hector,
back in his office mending brains or just using his copious
amounts of good sense. He was a smart man, Hector,
avoiding all the buzzwords and really caring. Too bad you
have to rent friends of his abilities or maybe it was best.
He had helped me see through my own evasion/denial
devices and that was not an easy task.

I wonder what he'd do in my situation? What about
the cops? I had a good relationship with the sheriff of Cal-
houn County, based on the fact I did him free ads when
he was running for reelection and he had a semiliterate's
appreciation of people who could write a coherent sentence. I say without shame that my headline for his elec-
tion day ad should stand as a classic of its kind: I'LL BUST
THEIR HEADS. LEGALLY. Sheriff Orton could keep No-Neck
off my back for the immediate present if only I could deal
with Bechman.

I took Bechman to bed with me and found no comfort
in him.

The next morning, I did the logical thing and went fishing. In truth, fishing may only prove that a man is smarter
than a fish but I found more meaning in it than that, in
the sense that I enjoyed the skills needed and took pride
in them and all the "stuff" that you used was good to the
hand. Environment, salt water, stress and strain, and careful selection took care of that. My big boat was a Grady-
White, North Carolina made, built to handle the stormy

seas around Cape Hatteras and I fished offshore in the summer when the weather patterns finally got straightened out and you could count on reasonably flat seas. The boat could withstand a great deal more than the skipper. I caught kingfish and dolphin and sharks and we released a very large percentage of what we caught since I've always felt the average Black Angus could beat the tastiest fish, no contest. I kept a smaller, sixteen-foot johnboat with a twenty-five-horsepower kicker for just pooting around the bay but today I wanted to use the big boat, just to feel the power.

I edged the twenty-five-footer up in the grass, making sure the tide was coming in, not out which could have left me stranded since the Grady-White rigged weighed something like four thousand pounds and you don't push that off a sandbar easily, and went wade fishing in jeans and sneakers, bait bucket and stringer trailing along in the current. I had picked a protected shore and the water was flat calm, disturbed by intriguing ripples and swirls and an occasional splash. I fished a popping cork and shrimp, elongated cork designed to imitate the sound of feeding fish when you twitched the rod, and I caught fish. Being by myself concentrated the mind, since I had nobody to talk to and concentration helps, don't tell me it doesn't. A positive attitude works too, I can't explain it, but it does.

Nobody had been at the slip when I launched, although I knew Mr. Evans had seen me hitch up the boat from his compound a hundred yards away. He'd be over for an afternoon drink and I wanted to tell him my problems. Hell, I wanted to tell the world my problems, if that would make them go away.

By midmorning, I had three fish injured in the catching process on the stringer and had released a couple more. Not a bad morning for me and I had felt safe the whole time. I had not seen another boat or human being and that was the main attraction of Point Lookout, although if you broke down you had to fix it or walk. I ran back in across a now-glassy bay, watching the herring gulls diving over a school of something and enjoying the drone of the big Yamahas on the stern.

"What you up to?" asked Evans, leaning out the window of his pickup to spit tobacco. Horrible habit. I wondered if his wife wanted to kiss him but had never had the courage to ask. He had nosed the pickup down the launch ramp so he could talk to me on the pier. He was short and wide and tough and long exposure to the sun had given him skin cancers which the local doctors burned off, leaving scabs and scars on his forearms and face. He wore a greasy blue gimmie cap with TAC insignia, which he had earned being a pilot in several wars, some of which we actually won. Unlikely person for Point Lookout or maybe not, since we also had a circus bear trainer in residence, not to mention the local characters that enliven any waterfront town. Why not an ex-fighter pilot?

"Nothing much," I said, voice changing a little as it always did, protective coloration or maybe imitation, "how 'bout you?"

"Same ol' sixes and sevens," he said, rubbing his crew cut which was largely nonexistent these days. He told me a sick astronaut joke which I had already heard. We got through the local pleasantries, discussed the weather, he asked about Margrit politely and I shrugged and he nodded quickly and waved good-bye. She fished like a fiend, strangely enough.

I tied up the boat, walked up the ramp vacated by Evans's truck, and got into Vince's van and drove to the nearest pay phone, some three miles down the road at the only store. The "Point Lookout Shopping Center" we called it but it had ice cream and fishing lures and good greasy hamburgers and you took your empty plate back to the kitchen to save the cook/waitress the walk. I called Vince collect and he was kind enough to accept the charges.

"Have you heard anything?" I asked.

"I checked it out, low profile," he said.

"And?"

"And nobody's really talking. It's bigger than the street creeps I know and there's that bank. They keep coming up. I didn't know it was a dirty bank." Vince sounded aggrieved that a bank could be dirty without his knowledge.

"Maybe it's not the whole bank."

"Maybe. I hear people have been through your office and there's word that a couple of mean-looking types are making the rounds of the clubs. My kind."

"No-Neck and Shorty."

"Could be. But they're looking. Asking a little, looking a lot. I kinda wish they'd come here."

"You don't want to get involved."

"*Su casa,*" he said abstractly.

"Bullshit! It's not your worry and I don't want you involved." I was actually lying, I think. If I had to involve somebody, Vince was a much better choice than most of the commercial artists and would-be Ad Biggies I ran with. Maybe I could throw Margrit to the thugs as a distraction.

"The chairman of the board, Mr. Bechman, will be down your way soon . . ." He broke off and asked where I was calling from.

"A pay phone. Bay City," I said, lying on purpose and hoping Vince picked it up.

"Well, Mr. Bechman is a fisherman. Not our kind, much more ree-fined. He's coming down farther south for *Poco Bueno.*"

"That's big bucks." *Poco Bueno* was a rich man's fishing tournament, organized by some wealthy and conservation-minded folks in the unlikely town of Port O'Connor, due south of my bayhouse. It drew the big boats, pro fishermen, expensive entries, millionaires, and hangers-on and the shrimpers and bait camps of Port

O'Connor took it in stride every year. I couldn't remember the entry list, invitation only, maybe fifty boats at a million bucks a boat average. One time a guy won it in a twenty-four-foot Scottie-Craft that he trailered in and all us real people applauded wildly.

Bechman would be a natural.

Vince told me he'd keep an ear open and asked me if I had any plans. I said I had the glimmering of an idea and I'd be calling and he asked me about the office and I explained how my friend was keeping the clients happy, I hoped. I went to the front of the store and asked what they had in the way of Marks-A-Lot and poster board. They surprised me with a more than adequate selection and I figured the farm schoolkids were a steady market. "Get the hay in and do your school poster," yellow-dog buses rolling down country roads at 6:00 A.M.

I went back to the phone with my purchases and called Vince again and asked him a specific question. He had to call and put me on hold and I waited, watching the tourists roar up to the store to mingle with the natives. It took me four years before I felt comfortable drawing my own cup of coffee from the big silver pot, four years and a lot of quiet talk. The weekend people tended to yell at the counter lady, as if she were slow. Vince came back on the line.

Yes, Bechman would be a natural for *Poco Bueno*.

12

Oʟ' Vɪɴᴄᴇ ᴡᴀs ᴀ ғᴏᴜɴᴛᴀɪɴ ᴏғ ɪɴ-
formation and the sports page of the *Victoria Advocate* did
the rest. The tournament would begin on Saturday morning and most of the contestants would drive—or fly—
down Friday. All I needed to know was when Bechman
was liable to leave the bank. Thank God the bank had got
into the austerity program recently and sold the airplane,
a veritable trend among corporations in oil-poor Houston.
Tuckerman had told me that sorrowfully and I missed him
briefly.

Houston was having a hard time adjusting to the yo-yo
pricing of the city's most desirable product. I suspect it
was even harder to get used to the idea that the city's
future, at least its rate of growth, depended on some Arabs
who had the temerity to play hardball with oil.

I was somewhat consoled to discover that the Arabs seemed no better at handling their game plan than we were. When the Saudis cut out from their self-imposed production restrictions they flooded the market and the price went down as fast as it had gone up a few years back. Faster, actually, disconcerting a whole bunch of good ole boys who had grown used to the best of everything, from call girls to corporate jets. Not to mention the Saudis, who sold twice the oil at half the price and ended up gaining zip.

Where oilmen used to drill holes in any piece of ground not actually occupied by humans, they now stacked rigs. Where they used to hold lavish parties, they now drank glumly in bars. Corporate art collections had enjoyed a miniboom and marketing departments tossed money around like water, all gone. I hated it because the up cycle of any economic roller coaster is much more fun than the plunge. Besides which, I had picked up my share and maybe a little more of the leavings from this very fat table, doing ads that surprised the oil world because they made sense without technotalk and looked good. Ah well.

Bechman would drive I hoped, since the only way into the sleepy little bayfront town of Port O'Connor was by small plane or car and flying a charter into Victoria made no sense since you faced a two-hour drive at the end of the flight. Vince said he owned a Suburban, black, the car of choice among high-roller fishermen. I sincerely hoped he would come alone.

Starting at nine o'clock Friday, I called Bechman on the half hour from the pay phone, ignoring the curious stares of the customers and nodding to people I knew. I made up a variety of names, changed my voice, got a lady from a bait camp to make the call for me and was told he was unavailable, in a meeting, away from his desk. Finally, at one-thirty, I was told he was out of the bank for the weekend.

I hopped in my van and headed for F.M. 172.

To get from Houston to Port O'Connor, you drive out U.S. 59 to Ganado (pronounced GA-'NAY-DAH by Texans) and hook a left onto F.M. 172 which is a lonely two-lane farm-to-market road. You drive south for about twenty-four miles to turn again and head around Matagorda and Lavaca bays to get to Port O'Connor. There is no better route, no more sensible way of doing it, although the best scenery available is cows and rice fields, with an occasional well as punctuation. Average speeds on 172 are well above seventy-five, with little black radar detectors on every dash.

I found a good spot, just south of "Crossroads," a full stop intersection featuring a country store which was open in no discernible pattern and had a big sign advertising fishing licenses they hadn't sold for three years. I pulled out the seven-by-fifty binoculars from the boat and settled down to wait, hood open and flashers going. I worried a little about the flashers draining the battery if I had to wait too long.

I was amazed at how many black cars and how many of the black cars were Blazers and Suburbans. It was hard to get a good view of the occupants and I had to wait until they slowed for the four-way stop before I was sure.

It was close to four when Bechman drove up, contemptuously slowing for the stop sign and accelerating past. I had about twelve miles in which to work. I waited until he was a mile or so ahead and then pulled out and floored the van.

Probably three of the twelve miles had gone past before I caught him, the van absolutely flat out and swaying badly as I roared past and his mouth was cussing me as I whipped on by. I held the pedal down and beat him to a slight dip in the road, handy grove of trees, a cattle guard over a dirt road into it, with about four or five minutes in hand. Out of the truck parked in the trees, lugging a card table and signs. Hammer the stakes into the ground, attach the signs, one a quarter mile ahead of the other and back to the table. I tried to look nonchalant as I dropped into my lawn chair, sunglasses on, beer on the table, and Bechman's truck came over the dip. I was out of breath, scared, and sweaty. I had placed the first sign practically in his lane and given him enough braking distance to stop before he got to my lawn chair and table. The signs read POCO BUENO PREREGISTRATION! ¼ MILE! and POCO BUENO REGISTER HERE! Nicely lettered, too.

I watched the hood of his truck and he whipped past the first sign and held off the stopping until the last minute. I saw the hood dip under the brakes, dragging the truck down, and waved him over lazily. He sat for a minute, waiting for me to come to the truck, and I waved again, holding up some papers. He switched off and got out.

"No one said anything about . . ." and I waved him over. He was within ten feet when he saw past the dark glasses and turned to get back to his Suburban and I beat him to the door and leaned against it, noting the CB antenna.

"Good to see you again!" I said.

"What do you want, Beaumont."

"As some friends of yours said to me not so very long ago, I just want a nice talk." I opened the front door and gestured him in. "Hop in, we'll go for a drive."

He stood there staring at me, lips compressed, eyes narrowed, probably wishing he had flown. He was fitted out in the best Abercrombie & Fitch had to offer, gentleman fisherman, except his legs were pasty white under the tailored khaki shorts. Practically hairless, too, which spoils the effect. He didn't move until I reached back and snapped off the CB antenna, not that the radio was any big threat but I wanted to impress him with my violence. Besides, the whippy steel antenna might be very persuasive.

I slashed it at his white legs. "Hop in, I said!"

I got into the back and he started up. I had him back down and collect my signs, card table, and chair, all of which went into the roomy back of the truck. I made sure he gave me the keys when he got out. He was planning to run and I reminded him that my legs were longer than his.

"Besides," I said, "I'm highly motivated."

When we got rolling finally, I had him set the cruise control at sixty, nice conservative, nonattention-attracting speed. I ignored his comments and suggestions. We went straight on 172 where you're supposed to turn for Port O'Connor and he grew visibly nervous, glancing over his shoulder at the road behind us as if there were an answer there. This was not a boardroom and I was dead serious. Even a mouse can be dangerous if cornered and I was considerably larger than a rodent and truly cornered.

When we got to Point Lookout and my house, I ushered him in and offered a drink which he declined. I sat him down at the little table and opened a cold beer for him without asking. He was not adjusting well to our situation and his eyes wandered around my modest cabin with disgust. If he had dusted the chair before he sat I would have punched him. I had made some of the furniture and the photos on the walls were important to me. The fishing rods had to hang somewhere, why not the living room? I found myself disliking him more in my environment.

"Bechman," I said. "What do you know about killing snakes?"

13

THE LITTLE BOAT WAS A TERRIBLE
tow and I was glad it was dark and I couldn't see it yaw-
ing and bouncing and taking water over the blunt square
bow. I don't know who invented the johnboat, it's everywhere now, but he never intended it to be towed at planing speeds in a chop. They're wonderful little boats,
capable of riding over a heavy dew practically, but they
are not intended for rough water. Mine was a sixteen-
footer, stable enough in the protected water of the bay,
but it was no match for the rolling wake of the Grady-
White and it lurched and bounced around in what star-
light there was, tugging at the half-inch nylon line I was
using as a tow rope. The nylon stretched enough to take
some of the yank out and that was good.

Bechman, even without his customary trappings of

power, had proven to be a tough cookie, sitting at my table, an unhappy guest. All he would say all afternoon was that I was going to jail, not a good prospect for a man with hemorrhoids. I had explained that he was unfairly and unjustly trying to wipe me out and he ignored all my carefully reasoned arguments as to why he should stop. We couldn't get to the meeting to plan the meeting. I had suspected this and finally quit trying to reason with him and read a book. He continued to sit at the table making threats. No Stockholm Syndrome was evident. I had a bruised hand to prove it, after he had announced he was walking out and I had to convince him he wasn't.

I felt good. Tough and in control, master of my own destiny for a change, a taker of action. My mind would edge back to that rotten motel and I'd yank it away and back to the present, my turf, my deal.

Both boats were down at the rotten old pier where Evans kept *his* johnboat, away from anybody. If Evans wondered why I had both boats in the water, he hadn't said anything. At dusk, Bechman and I walked down to the pier and I had escorted him into my big boat, tossed off the lines, and headed for the Gulf, some fourteen miles away. He wasn't speaking to me now.

Actually, the wind and water were fine and I wished I were going through the jetties on a normal fishing trip. Seas were two-to-four and I probably would have started picking up kings within five miles. Bechman appeared fairly comfortable with the boat even though I suspected he was used to much larger craft, with pro captains and a mate to bring him drinks. I asked him if he had done much sailing and he shook his head. When we cleared the slop at the mouth, wind and tide pushing the water up into big rollers, compressed by the twin granite arms of the jetties, he was visibly less at ease. The nighttime did it to you because you couldn't really see the rollers and adjust accordingly. The johnboat was terrible in tow in the waves and I came off plane and creeped due south away from the traffic lanes, the shrimpers, and all normal commercial boats.

It took forever to get where I wanted, about seven miles off Cavallo Pass, as isolated a spot of Gulf water as I could think of. The nighttime and the slow pace made it seem as if we were much farther off.

"Bechman," I said, "I wish you'd listen to reason."

He snorted: "Kidnapping is a federal offense."

"Not until forty-eight hours and I'm gonna say you stole my boat," I said.

He threw up his hands and stared at the waves he couldn't see. I had stripped the johnboat and it was bare, no anchor, no line, no paddle, no nothing. I handed Bechman a quart oil can with the top cut out and my hand-held VHF radio.

"You'll probably have to bail," I said. "I hope the cold front doesn't come through tonight like they say it is. Because it gets awful out here, the bottom slopes up so fast."

I motioned for him to get into the johnboat and he looked at me like I was crazy. I picked him up by the shirt front, finally getting his shirttail out of his pants. He was much too tailored for my taste anyway.

"You would prefer to swim, maybe?"

It took threats and tough talk and a shove or two but he finally came to the conclusion that I meant it and stumbled into the johnboat. He stared at me wildly, the first time I had seen him ruffled, and who could blame him? Alone in a ridiculous and inadequate boat, far out at sea, the middle of the night, hardly Bechman's territory. His hair was messed up by the wind and he looked old.

"I've had the big radio on all the way out and there's nobody within range of it," I shouted to him. "So I wouldn't waste the batteries calling Mayday." He looked at the walkie-talkie blankly and I told him he was forty-five miles from the Coast Guard station and to forget that too.

"Your best bet is tomorrow evening. Maybe a shrimper will come this way, although most of them are Mexican and don't speak English. How's your Spanish?"

"You can't leave me!" he said in shock.

"You can have me killed but I can't leave you," I said. "Right."

"We weren't going to . . ." his voice trailed off and he looked at the walkie-talkie again.

"That's a good little gadget," I said. "Good for picnics and stuff. But it's only good for a couple of miles with fresh batteries. So if you want to talk, you'd better make up your mind before I'm out of range." I looked up at my eight-foot antenna. "You might get three miles," I said. "I don't remember the last time I changed the batteries."

With that, I wheeled the boat around and roared off, using more throttle than necessary to throw a good wash his way. He could start bailing immediately. I checked the loran and memorized the numbers so I could get back to his location in a hurry. I had set the walkie-talkie on Channel 72 and I waited until I was a mile or two away before calling him. I held the mike far away from my face so it would sound faint.

"Bechman," I said, "remember to keep track of the current. You wouldn't want to drift down to Mexico." I popped the microphone a couple of times and listened.

Garbage. More threats, questions, you can't do this, I'll have you hanged, we have laws, insults, and finally a silence. I waited, idling around in a circle, the bow lifting up and splitting an unseen wave almost silently. The big Yamahas on the back were virtually noiseless. What an asshole. They don't hang you in Texas.

Then he said, "Beaumont?" I kept quiet. "Bechman calling Beaumont, Bechman calling Beaumont, come in please." I kept quiet. His transmissions were sporadic and

I suspected he was trying to start the twenty-five-horse-power Johnson on the johnboat. It was good exercise but futile, since I had broken off the electrodes on the spark plugs. They would look fine from the outside but there was no way that motor would start. I flipped off the navigation lights and eased the Grady-White in his direction, worrying that he'd panic and fall out of the boat. I wanted him to call. I was nervous in the dark.

I kept moving slowly and silently in his general direction with the radio volume turned up high. If he didn't call soon, I'd have to go back to find out what happened to him and I didn't have a Plan B. Had he dropped the radio in the water?

I divided my attention between the loran and the radio, fiddling with the squelch and trying to resist the temptation to call him. A shrimper came in on 72 with a bunch of rapid-fire Spanish and I wanted to tell him to shut up.

I heard Bechman call him. "Attention! Attention! Bechman calling . . . shrimper! Attention!"

I keyed the mike and made garbage noises with my mouth, trying to imitate radio squawk. I heard the Mexican skipper suggest they switch channels and hoped my more powerful radio and tall antenna were letting me hear stuff Bechman couldn't on the hand-held set. I heard him call a couple more times and then another pause. His transmissions were getting stronger and I slowed the boat to idle, not wanting to run up on him in the dark. The loran confirmed we were close.

"Beaumont? Beaumont are you there?"

I figured I had done enough.

I picked up the mike and said very softly, "Motor Vessel Futility calling Bechman. Bechman, do you read me?"

"Oh Jesus God," he said, "where are you?"

"Your transmission's garbled," I said softly. "Please wait." I waited five minutes by my watch and picked up the mike and said, "Beaumont calling Bechman. Calling Bechman, come in please."

I sincerely hoped the FCC wasn't listening to us fracture radio procedures out in the Gulf. The Mexican skipper was back on 72 and I could catch about every fifth word. Bechman came on in bursts between the Spanish, "Come back . . . how far . . . talk . . . please . . . Beaumont . . . hear me?"

"Bechman," I said. "Are you ready to play fair?"

14

W<small>E HAD A NICE TALK, OUT IN THE</small> blackness of the night, a zillion stars gleaming overhead and I took scant comfort from them. I felt even smaller than the display in the sky normally made one feel, knowing that I had made myself into something I didn't want to examine too closely, Bechman's pathetic display hurting me and my sense of self as much as his.

He was only alone out there for forty-five minutes or thereabouts but I was all too aware of the diminished sense of importance an indifferent sea would bring and the black night made it that much worse. Had my engines hiccupped, I would have probably wet my pants, so tiny and afraid. And I was in a big boat with radio, loran, all the rest. Of course, I wasn't used to being so powerful nothing would touch me. And imagination is the deadliest threat of all.

I had almost run him over, the johnboat blending with the waves and only his shouts above the quiet murmur of my engines steering me the last few hundred feet. I hit him with the hand-held Q-beam, a hundred thousand candlepower lancing out to catch him, bedraggled and sweaty-wet, balanced in the tiny boat. Maybe he'd be okay when memory and rationalization worked to smooth down the rough edges of his "ordeal," broken in three quarters of an hour!

I wouldn't let him aboard my boat.

I tossed him a line and had him hold it to keep our boats attached and told him what I wanted, then tested the little Jap cassette recorder, gave a time and date and place for the tape, and let him talk.

He spoke corporatese, never saying it straight, and he would not admit to any of my trauma, saying he didn't know about "that side of it." But someone did and Bechman had approved and thus he found himself wet and afraid in the Gulf rather than sampling the lush pickings available for *Poco Bueno* participants, the finest food and luscious suntanned girls all ready. I debated trying for a fuller confession, judging as best I could, standing behind the wheel ready to reverse the line from his hands should he start to regain lost ground. I had to actually twitch my boat away once when he faltered in his narrative and he was pathetically anxious to make amends when he felt the rope pulling from his hands.

I had nothing legal, of course, and scarcely cared because I wasn't really interested in proving anything in a court. But I had CEO Bechman explaining that he had authorized or was at least aware that thugs were in his service. Said thugs had attacked me (again with his implied consent) because I had seen "confidential papers" relating to (this took the tug on the line) "American Title Investment Group, Inc.," and that would be enough to give the reporting dogs plenty of meat. I ran the tape back and checked it a couple places to make sure it had recorded right and slipped the cassette into my pocket.

My overall impression was that he had graduated from one of those seminars where they teach businessmen "How to Deal with the Press." A couple of times, I said, "Aw shit. Did you or didn't you?" And he still evaded.

I had wanted to ask him whom he worked for really, planning how to phrase the question, but his tape-recorded mumblings in the night made me feel queasy and I decided it was not important.

Too much Bechman, too much everything.

I pulled him over and let him aboard, watching for any last-minute rushes, but Bechman wanted no more of this night and place and was eager to help me secure the johnboat and get on our way. He actually chatted a little on the long trip home, slow because I couldn't put the big boat up on plane until we were inside the jetties. Shared experience. Mind's a wonderful thing, I guess.

In the smooth water of the bay, almost glassy now, I cut the running lights to give my eyes every break and we hummed home at a good clip. I stood at the wheel to watch for crab-trap buoys and let him enjoy the ride.

Into a silence he asked, "Would you really have left me out there?" and I thought it most merciful to tell him yes.

We came back to the pier and secured the boats, Bechman helping with the lines although I checked his knots, and walked a silent walk up to my house. Evans's pickup was off to the side and that was unusual and I wondered for a moment if he was there to borrow some whiskey, town and liquor stores twenty nighttime miles away and closed to boot since it was late. Evans was sitting at my table, chair pushed back, the shotgun from the pickup's rack across his knees. I remembered when he told me he had replaced the customary rifle with the scattergun, complaining about his eyes.

He had a glass of my whiskey in front of him.

And on the floor, not very comfortable with my indoor-outdoor carpeting, were my old friends No-Neck and Shorty. I wondered how long they'd been in that position. It would be nice to know where they came from, maybe they followed Bechman around like puppies. But they were here and I remembered the office and shuddered.

It explained Bechman's capitulation and near-courtesy. I suspect his brain was running full with plans for me once he was back on dry land and in command of his now-reclining army.

Evans said, "You had some visitors."

"Looks like you caught 'em in the act," I replied.

"Well, I keep an eye out, you know." And he had the grace to blush, tough old goat. He once had confessed to me, better part of a bourbon bottle in his gut, that he had noticed Margrit changing clothes a time or two through our unshaded windows and it "made his vision blur." I'd never known a more welcome Peeping Tom and I looked at Bechman, who was gray and sweaty all of a sudden. Bullit came slinking up from the bushes and rattled on the door glass with her claws.

"You just earned another trip out into the Gulf," I said to Bechman, and he looked sick.

"Beaumont," said Evans. "You're letting the VC inside the wire and that can get you hurt." His tone was mildly reproving, like the time I hit the pier. I would have tied and handcuffed the two of them, Evans didn't feel like he needed to. He sipped my whiskey and his eyes didn't move and I shoved Bechman to the couch. Bullit hit the door again and I let her in and she sniffed at the guys on the floor cautiously. Then she went over under Evans's chair and slumped down. He scratched her head between the ears with stubby fingers, the backs of his hands showing pink peeling places where the doctor had burned off skin cancers.

"Now what am I gonna do?" I said to the world.

"Sheriff Orton be glad to detain them for you. I didn't want to search them, but if they're not carryin', I expect we can supply something." I felt like a virgin. Evans acted like he was bored. Of course, the folks in Point Lookout were more elemental than I. When they had trouble with a prowler, not Evans peeking at Margrit but a petty thief-type prowler, they got the guy cornered in a field and sprayed it with shotgun blasts, not meaning to wound, Evans had explained, but to let him know they were serious. It worked.

"Bechman," I said, "when are you going to quit this shit?"

"That the head knocker?" asked Evans with interest. Then he began to tell me about killing a snake by cutting off its head and I began to laugh, offending the old boy slightly, but the meaning was not lost on Bechman who motioned me out to the porch.

"You have my solemn word," he started, and I showed him the tape. "And that too, of course, all I want to be is rid of this entire affair, I can guarantee no further difficulty . . ."

He talked too much, wordy reassurances, and I was tempted to turn Evans loose but afraid of the tortures that he might think up and Bechman must have felt the same because he kept glancing back inside the house, not your usual boardroom enemies these, and I was struck with how quickly Evans would commit, no hesitation about whose side he was on or who might sue or what.

"Can you call off the dogs?" I asked, jerking a thumb at my opponents on the floor.

"Of course, they work for me."

"You know their names, then?"

"Naturally."

"And how they're paid, how much?" He nodded.

I pulled out the tape recorder and bowed. "Talk," I said, inserting the cassette and running down to the end of his previous spiel. I was interested to learn that Shorty did make more than No-Neck and both could be hired for account executive wages, no big deal, maybe I'd get my own private army. Maybe I'd hire No-Neck just to have him fix drinks.

Bechman didn't like going into detail and glared even more when I added his name and title to the end of the tape. Tough. I went back inside and bent over the pair on the floor and did my best to do a careful frisk, like a TV cop show, staying out of Evans's line of fire. He moved clear to make sure they were covered, Bechman staying on the porch, and I came up with a roll of quarters, two small pocketknives, and wallets.

"They must of thought I'd be easy pickings," I said to Evans, and he laughed.

"Come join us," I yelled to Bechman, still out on the porch. He hesitated and then moved off.

"Let 'em up," I said to Evans. Surely Bechman wouldn't do something stupid.

Evans moved his shotgun out of position slightly and I told the two to get up. They sorted themselves out quickly, No-Neck starting to bluster some, and I waved him quiet and addressed Shorty, who was really a "Courtland."

"Do they call you Court?" I asked, and he nodded.

"Well look, there's been a mistake and there's no reason for us to fight anymore. Mr. Bechman said it, on tape, and he's the boss, right?" The nod was slow in coming and I remembered the brick wall at my back from long ago and wanted no more grievances here. They handled me easily enough under orders, I wanted no part of them if they were personally motivated.

"You'd win," I said to Court, and moved forward with my hand and he shook after a time and I repeated the gesture with No-Neck, a "Henry," and offered them both a drink. I wanted to make friends.

Outside we heard the Suburban start up with a roar and Bechman slammed it into gear and yanked it through my yard on his exit, leaving ruts with the heavy truck that would be hell to fill. Wasn't very loyal of him, I thought.

"Looks like I need to give you guys a ride to the bus station," I said. "Guess he didn't like the company."

"Naw," said Courtland. "We have our own car. Just stopped for gas and Mr. Hotshot got ahead of us. He doesn't have to pay for his tickets."

"Or insurance," said No-Neck.

"I need another touch of whiskey," Evans remarked.

We had drinks and they wanted to know a bit about fishing, taking their cues from the color photos on the wall, Beaumont with kingfish, Beaumont at the helm, Margrit topless in the boat, dreamy and pretty, I shouldn't have had it on the wall. But only friends had been here before.

Evans said to nobody, "I can't stand an officer who leaves his men, there's no excuse for that." And he drove us slowly to their car and then my truck, parked in the grove of trees on 172, and never said another thing about the whole incident.

Shorty mentioned he'd be seeking new employment soon and I was glad. No-Neck said something about Margrit and looked at me with an obvious challenge and I just shrugged. I hoped they'd enjoy the fishing tournament and they said Bechman had them bartending mostly. Court said something about messing up my office and I waved it off, glad it wasn't me. We didn't talk about the stat camera. I was glad to see them go.

I turned the lights out and put my feet up and had a drink which I richly deserved. I envied Evans and the way everything was clear for him, clear choices and a direct reaction, no second, third, fourth, and fifth thoughts. Maybe he could hide his fears.

Saturday evening I watched fishless from the boat as

the *Poco Bueno* fleet came thundering through the jetties, big boats, antennae whipping in the wind, fish flags flying, throwing spray and radio chatter everywhere, a good time was had by all, calm seas, clear water, and a bright future ahead. Me too, I thought.

Anybody can make a mistake.

15

I FELT I COULD GO TO THE OFFICE Monday without fear, just like real people, and some of the events of the past few days began to fade. I kissed a glad-to-be-back Tammy on the tip of her nose and promised her the damnedest lunch she'd ever had and she impishly said something semisexy about the offensive backfield in the cafeteria and I stared, unable to think of something clever. Made me nervous, not that it meant anything. I called my clients, one by one, and my old ad agency buddy had done them proud, dazzling with his PC printouts of audience ratings here and showing billing footwork like you wouldn't believe there, especially since most of the time he had to be acting in ignorance. I send him two bottles of Maker's Mark and my heartfelt thanks.

He hadn't even tried to steal the clients, which made me wonder. I think I was hurt.

Tammy and I went, her choice, to the premier steak-house in the city, decorated in Corpus Christi 1958, and she explained that she always wanted to see "where the fat cats played." I'm afraid it was a disappointment, not the steaks which sizzled satisfactorily, huge mounds of meat cooked to perfection, but the oilmen. From the suits, I'd guess that most of the patrons were bankruptcy law-yers and the few good ole boys wore expressions of suspi-cion and clutched their bourbons tightly. I noticed the waitresses scrutinizing the American Express cards care-fully, too. Times were hard.

Tammy was a sweet smart ass. She more than held her own in conversation and I found myself watching her as if she were a brand-new person, even though I'd known her since she was a kid, an "older" friend of my daughter's, full of eleven-year-old secrets and very respectful, good manners, what the hell did they talk about so endlessly, the time she spent the night, with giggles all night long?

"Sex," she said. "What else?"

"Little girls aren't supposed to . . ."

"Come *on*, Beaumont!" she said, eyeing the last bite on my plate. I gave it to her and she accepted without hesita-tion.

"I remember one of the James Bond books when he was eating with the bad guy, stone crabs drowned in but-ter according to Fleming, and the bad guy tells Bond that they had eaten better than anyone in the country," she said. "That's how I feel now."

And she kissed me lightly on the mouth for thanks.

The Xerox man came and we put the typewriter in the closet since we had more typewriters than people and the mess at home was calling. I got things organized, debated calling the bank, and then decided I might as well go full speed, so I had Tammy send the insertion orders and the time buys. I really didn't think Bechman would cancel the ad program now, since I had an excellent argument against it in the desk drawer. I made an extra cassette too and mailed it to a friend out of town, with instructions not to open the envelope unless I got clobbered.

I told Tammy I was off, Bullit frolicking around and pawing the door, and she came up to me and kissed me again, thank you, and I was conscious of her firm softness pressed against me.

Then she leaned out the door before I started up Vince's van and said, "Beaumont. I'm twenty-five." She disappeared before I could reply.

What could I say?

I walked right up to my door and let myself in, glad I didn't have to sneak through the fence, and there was no mess. Even the poor TV was back in my credenza and Margrit was in my bed asleep. She looked wonderful sleeping and that is hard to do.

I stood there watching. Her hair was pulled back and controlled and her face was peaceful, sheet swelling over her breasts, how many hands had? One foot had poked out under the covers and I knelt quietly and began kissing her painted toes and she woke up smiling and pulled me on top of her and began with considerable fervor to touch and bite and rip the clothes off me, nipples taut and mouth a little sour from sleep but hot and everywhere, and I was quick as a teenager, moods shifting like mad, dominant and angry now and then succumbing to her insistence, and she was Margrit, there's none like her, never will be.

"What a nice way to come home," she said softly, cuddled close, the sweet musty scent of her drifting in the room and I smoked in silence, bitter thoughts scurrying through my mind and surfacing just enough to turn me sour. I didn't want to be postcoital and she had loved me now without reservation and what's a man to do?

"You make a good movie?"

"I made a bad movie, a very bad movie, but I got paid."

"How much?"

"Not enough but I could see why when I got there. You wanta hear about it?" Slow, sexual smile.

"Yes. No."

"I'll tell you when it will do us both some good, it's not so bad as all that," she said, clutching me possessively. "Can we sleep a little now?"

Her breathing slowed and she maintained her clutch softly, tightening her grip when I shifted to put out the cigarette. I lay there and wondered what would become of me and wondered about Tammy. Strange male beast we carry, thinking about one girl with another pressed against you. Still Tammy had changed or was changing and I wondered what it meant. I decided it was best not to think of her too much, twenty-five or not.

I slept for a little and when I woke up she was in the shower, cleanliness is next to something-or-other. Margrit wanted steak and I wanted lasagna. We had steak.

In four hours we were at each other's throats and she flounced out mad, unforgivable insults bouncing from the walls, and I remembered she'd be going home to an electricityless apartment and followed her after a couple of minutes.

It was hot in her apartment and our bodies slipped across each other's and when I woke up I had an awful crick in my back and she must have slept with her feet in my mouth.

I used her toothbrush, what the hell, and wondered about Mexican diseases. I'd drive downtown to HL&P tomorrow and get her lights turned on and maybe that would make up for some of the stuff which came out of my mouth when I was mad.

She looked wonderful sleeping in the heat.

16

I HAD THREE WHOLE DAYS OF NOR-
malcy before all roofs everywhere fell in. Damn, I was
efficient, snapping out commands, writing my charming
letters on yellow pads to an extent that Tammy claimed
her typewriter wanted overtime, conceptualizing and selling, and I had time left over to call Margrit's number and
hear the phone buzz away in an empty apartment.

Where the *hell* was she?

Tammy, wearing a worried frown, brought me the
morning papers on Thursday. I put aside the morning edi-
tion of the evening paper as I had every morning for the
last nine hundred mornings because I wanted to read the
evening paper in the *evening*, the hell with circulation
claims and competitive spirit, no matter when they threw
it on the lawn.

She had folded the paper back to show me an item of news that made me very nervous indeed. Bechman had unexpectedly resigned, citing "ill health," and I wondered if that were current or future. I couldn't imagine the snooty bastard quitting if he wasn't forced out.

It made my cassettes useless, I suppose.

I worked on at somewhat impaired efficiency and couldn't decide who I should call at the bank. All the Bechman replicas were nameless in my memory. I wasn't sure what to do and I always do nothing under those circumstances which contradicts another adage: "Do something, even if it's wrong." I had my head buried ostrichlike in an annual report copy draft (pointing with pride and viewing with alarm) when I looked out of my ground-floor window and saw the world's largest limo at the curb. I mean I've seen stretch limos before but this one looked like the work of Plasticman.

Tammy came in with a business card, nine-pound stock, creamy ivory in color, elegant engraved typeface, "Lois Harthorne." I raised a brow and she pantomimed to the reception area, making bowing gestures of extreme respect.

"Well hell," I said. "Show her in."

"Them, Boss, them." She had never called me Boss before.

I was standing when the lady swept in accompanied by the largest single man I'd ever seen outside the Houston Oilers' locker room. She took in my office with a glance, not blanching at the bare-breast-in-silhouette photo behind my desk, which was a treasure three successive secretaries had tried to get me to remove, or the crudely carved Mexican fish hanging from the ceiling. She sat, nodded to me, and took out a cigarette, which the huge guy lighted. He pulled his chair back six inches so he could sit down, lighter poised. I shoved an ashtray across the desk, dumping the butts first. It was the least I could do.

Ms. Harthorne wore an elegant dress which I suppose would better be described as a gown and it was a lovely pale ivory like the business card and it matched her dusky skin tones perfectly. She was probably the most beautiful woman I'd ever seen, including every model I've ever flirted with. She made Margrit look like an awkward, if attractive, child. No trace of accent, formal phrasing, a quiet monotone with black, black eyes looking directly at me. It was impossible to think of her in the context of concrete overcoats. But maybe that's why she was successful. She certainly looked successful.

"Mr. Beaumont," she said, "I have precisely three minutes."

"Including travel time?"

"I understand you're (A) not intimidated and (B) quite a wit," she said. "May I go directly to the heart of the matter?"

"Please," I said.

"I know more about you and your . . . organization . . . than I could possibly desire. However, your handling of the Bechman problem, that is, 'problem' from your perspective, of course, indicates that (A) you are a man of imagination and (B) my own suppliers suffer from weak leadership."

"I saw you took care of the leadership problem, problem from your perspective, already," I said. She arched a delicate eyebrow and I pulled the paper out of my wastebasket.

"I never read the newspapers," she said dismissively.

"So what may I do for you Ms. . . . ." I picked her card up and studied it.

"You may (A) go to work for me or (B) be put out of business." She put out the cigarette and the silent man picked up the ashtray and emptied it immediately and put it back.

"I always was good at multiple-choice tests," I said, and nobody smiled. "But I don't think I want to go to work for you. I'm afraid of heights. And the tests usually had 'none of the above' as an option."

"Mr. Beaumont," she said, "you have no options. I have a number of things an enterprising and clever person might do for me. Speech writing. Political things. I want you to become employed by my organizations." And she nodded once more before leaving with a flourish. The large fellow had every door open before she got there and the giant car was away before I organized my next smart crack.

The phone rang and she was calling from the car, "Mr. Beaumont. Please indicate your agreement to this number." And the man's voice came on, it must have been the bodyguard/valet, and he gave me a number. I wrote it down immediately, no use taking chances. Tammy came in while I was trying to make a paper airplane from the business card, tough work because it was too thick. My lady of all work was impressed.

"Did you see the guy?"

"What guy?" I asked.

"The guy who . . . oh shit! Who were they?"

I handed her the creased business card and shrugged. She was awfully impressed. "Jeez, he was wonderful."

I looked at her, blonde and pretty even with the god-awful hairdo, young, firm, and sure she was untouchable. How do any of them ever survive?

"Size isn't everything, Tam."

"I know, I know, of course. But he was *huge.*" I think he had tapped something deep in her psyche and hoped she didn't hang around sports bars. Her hands were shaking slightly.

"Tammy. Stop your fantasies. Save it."

"What did they want?"

"Why," I said, "it's simple. They want to put you out of a job."

She left to moon over her typewriter and devote her energy to fantasy and I was unreasonably jealous, or is that redundant? I didn't want my Tammy to be impressed by an outsized thug when grace, wit, and charm, not to mention veteran sexual prowess, lived in the next office. Damnit, she was mine even if she wasn't and I got caught up in the old possession number, the genetic heritage that all shrinks were so against, claiming it was the root cause of destroyed relationships and unhappiness and bad skin probably, but I indulged myself nevertheless.

It takes an essential blind arrogance to give short shrift to a system bred into us anyhow. I suspected their assumptions. I was much too upset about Tammy's lusting, too, and that was disturbing in itself.

Ms. Harthorne meant what she said. Ms. Harthorne took herself seriously and if the trappings of her entrance were any indicator, I suspect she had at least the money clout to be a problem. Why couldn't I stay out of other people's papers and I'll never have to worry about the little jerk or his cocaine again, terrible way to think of the dead, working for her doing what? Political work. Speech writing. Swat the fly. Did I know more than I knew I knew? Or was she just impressed by my wit and personality?

I didn't call the number.

You don't get to make clear, simple decisions. At least I didn't. I had drifted into the agency business on my own because I wanted to die and was devoting my energies to doing just that via bourbon and didn't have time to play the big agency game for somebody else. I was doing famously at that, working half time with most afternoons blurry, thanks to double bourbon on the rocks, but I had a good life and seventeen ties. When the meetings and the procedures and the people began to be too much, I had almost casually quit and got myself a hole-in-the-wall office and some letterheads and today I am an agency owner. Somehow, I got the bourbon under control, thanks to Hector more than anything, and had inched up every year until I had some impressive accounts payable figures.

I spent more on office supplies last year than I billed in my first three months as an agency.

The work wasn't that hard. People are essentially rational in their buying decisions and who the hell knows what advertising really does anyhow? I liked direct-response stuff, where you could count coupons and really *see* the results of your toil, but most advertising efforts weren't like that. Nonetheless, if you could figure out what the client had to offer that was worthwhile and communicate this clearly in the appropriate media *and* get the resulting ads or spots or mailers or campaign past the built-in problems of all-too-human clients: pride and I've got to change something to prove I exist and what is the competition doing, if you could accomplish all that, you had a chance to get results.

Which was fun. No backing up to the pay window.

If you were careful or an economic coward, you could make money at it too. It had been a long time since I took home less than sixty grand and I didn't really work too hard. Being small meant you dealt with the dregs of advertising, clients with no training or insight into the business, and you certainly had to deal with their foibles but sixty grand is sixty grand and my kids appreciated it, as did their mother, gone away now and not happily, who could blame her.

I tossed the business card but I kept the number. I didn't think I'd forget Ms. Harthorne quickly. It was too quiet and I went out and Tammy had her sweet blonde head down on her typewriter.

"I'll get you an autograph," I said. "But will you please do the accounts payable summary first?"

17

IN ONE MORNING MY BUSINESS EVAP-
orated. Now you see it, now you don't.

I had left early the evening before, Tammy still busy
being busy, and gone to the Foxy Lady to see about my
car and return the van. I didn't really want to know about
the van.

"This crazy woman came by," I said to Vince, "and
scared me to death."

He looked. Vince is good at that, nonverbal communications skills, there should be a course in it. He had driven
me down to the police compound and we had retrieved
the Corvette. A car-cost of one scratched fender, from the
tow truck I expect, seemed reasonable enough. Thirty-
eight bucks plus ten dollars a day storage seemed unrea-
sonable, but I paid it with a smile.

I had had exactly seventeen hundred dollars to give back to him plus a three-hundred-dollar personal check and I felt like I had got away with murder, moneywise. Vince refused interest payments and we both were a touch awkward over the money. He had listened to my tale of high jinks on the high seas with a deadpan expression and I probably made it seem more glamorous than it was. I paused for a second and told him the truth.

"It made me feel like shit. I don't like the guy or even that type of guy but nobody should get that scared."

"It was good he had the heavies waiting. Saves you guilt."

"It was better Mr. Evans was there with trusty shotgun," I replied.

"Yeah. But it takes you off the hook, headwise."

We both watched one of the girls bouncing around the stage, feigning extreme sexual passion, and it looked like a six-year-old dancing the "dirty bop" which dates me. We were too close and Vince had no illusions left, maybe it was catching. He scanned the crowd and shook his head and we had another round. Tomato juice for Vince.

"I don't know your elegant lady," he said after the girl was down to a white crotch covering and the music climaxed. "I've never heard of her. You want to stay away from American Title Investment Group, though, bad news."

"All these years," I said. "All these years, I've been reasonably happy and productive and I barely had heard of them. I plan on continuing this great tradition."

We touched glasses and he left and I got into a long conversation, about babies, God help me, with little Saki, one of Vince's dancers. Chinese-American, golden brown all over, and nice. She said she was just being friendly and no need to buy her one of those dumb drinks but I insisted, figuring she could use the money. I didn't know what infants could see, was it blurs or colors and could they even see color? I told her what I had read about fish and how blind many of them are but it didn't seem to satisfy her baby curiosity.

"Got any pediatricians that come in here?" I asked.

"They wouldn't admit it if they did," she said ruefully.

She was a nice girl and had consoled me in the past and we walked a delicate line between customer and friends, semisuccessfully. She hustled me, sure, out of reflex maybe, but she'd always let me know, a grin and a wink, when she was about to do it and I could choose. She was a friend.

I closed the place down and went home relatively sober and alone and no Margrit to answer the phone at her place. This "marriage" did not appear to be made in heaven.

The next morning things went nuts.

The answering service and half a page of messages at nine in the morning and my home builder was going in-house with his advertising, an odd decision since nobody there knew a Velox from chicken pox. My commercial real estate guy didn't want the series of direct mail pieces and the grocery store chain had eliminated me from the semifinals in the competition for their account. The printer whom I was paying five thousand a month on account wanted all his money now. The oil field services people put their stuff on hold because of oil prices and the insurance company didn't need an annual report, after all.

Tammy got in on some of this, standing shocked against my office wall and listening, and I kept my voice steady throughout each conversation, let the wolves know that you're afraid and they come ripping in, tearing at the bloody flesh.

"I think we can forget the accounts payable for a while," I said to the room.

We left early for lunch and didn't say anything, the American Express folks hadn't canceled yet but they were in Phoenix and there's a time difference so we'd better get lunch quick. I was in a state of shock and wished Tammy wasn't with me so I didn't have to be so strong.

"Has this ever happened before?" she asked quietly, after the better part of a big glass of straight vodka-on-ice had vanished down my throat. This was not a time for gentle drinking.

"Sweetie," I said. "Oh shit, I'm not supposed to say that. Ah . . . to the best of my knowledge, this has never happened before in the history of advertising. Certainly not to me."

"Do you think . . ."

"I think it's the broad."

"Don't call her that!"

"You're right. She obviously deserves more respectful treatment. I believe we can begin to see . . . faintly . . . the fine hand of Ms. Harthorne at work here." I waved for more vodka.

"Getting drunk doesn't help," she said.

"There's not enough booze to get me drunk right now," I said. "This is shock treatment."

"So is she," Tammy muttered.

"Hi!" said Margrit cheerfully. "I've been looking for you!" I'm glad I wasn't a gunfighter because she slipped up without my ever seeing her. My haunts were well established, of course, the middle-age disease again. She slipped into the chair next to mine and put her hand possessively on my arm. Tammy withdrew thirty feet without moving an inch. They exchanged pleasantries and I waved for more vodka.

"What are you guys doing . . . drinking lunch?"

"I'm through," said Tammy. "Let me take your car back to the office so I can answer the phones."

I handed her my keys with an imploring look and she smiled whitely at Margrit and left. Margrit stayed where she was, little pats and rubbings, all excited, glowing, and I never saw her more attractive.

"You're not going to believe this," she whispered, "neither do I!"

"What?"

"I've got the most fabulous job!"

"I thought you were a movie star these days."

"Oh no, I had to do that and it will never be released, I bet. Good stories, something to remember in my old age, but the job is incredible and they came to me!"

"Dancing at Vince's."

"No, a *real* job," she said.

"Well, congratulations." I felt bad and hugged her. Why should she be miserable? "I'm proud of you," I said. "What's the job, what do you do?"

"There's this wonderful lady, I'm her personal and private secretary, my own office and somebody to type for me, just the really confidential stuff is what I handle, my own business cards!"

"Who's the wonderful lady?" I asked, knowing the answer.

"She's amazing. If you meet her, you won't believe her. God, she's beautiful, just a touch dyke-y, you know." She lit a cigarette and sipped my drink, made a face and asked one of the waitresses for a glass of white wine. "I can handle that," she said. "I've never had business cards before."

"Who's the wonderful lady?"

"Wait just a minute. I'll travel all over and she's arranged a suite next to hers at the Warwick Hotel so I don't have to pay rent! That's like another five hundred a month!"

"Margrit," I said. "Who are you working for?"

The waitress came with the check and I couldn't compute the tip, something that is as natural to me as breathing. I couldn't figure 20 percent of twenty-eight dollars.

"It's a wonderful company—very confidential—and my boss, the lady, is Ms. Harthorne. She's in charge."

"Margrit," I said, "*I* would have made business cards for you." I looked at the patient waitress, "Maybe we'd better open another tab."

To Margrit's stubborn head, I tried an explanation, raining on the parade as usual, damn the cynic. It was doomed from Word One. At about Word Fifty, she interrupted to tell me I was a sicko paranoid who thought the world revolved around himself and Ms. Harthorne had an *executive search* firm seek her out. Then she stormed out, not finishing her wine.

I told the waitress to leave it, I'd take care of it.

18

I HAD STARTED THE BUSINESS WITH A case of Old Crow and a thousand dollars with six thousand in reserve, profit sharing from the big agency. My accounts payable list, typed this time, was one hundred forty-six thousand, seven thirty-eight and change.

Against this I had about twenty-six thousand in the bank which I went to verify only to discover that Tammy had paid some agency bills, including American Express, and the twenty-six thou was really twenty-two. Plus maybe ten thousand in a money market account and eighty to ninety owed me and this snowball *had* to keep rolling. The economics of the agency business are such that you lived on the float, collecting from your clients quickly and dragging your feet a little paying suppliers. Everybody expected it and you got sixty days without a whimper. Things changed quickly when you got past ninety and heaven help you if there was even a rumor about bad times. Nervous business.

Why do you think we drove fancy cars and ran up big restaurant tabs?

If this month's billing didn't come in—which it couldn't if I had no work—all of the sixty-day-old accounts payable would inexorably slide into the ninety-day column and the phone would ring its little heart out and I didn't know what I'd say to these people. The ninety-day folks would talk to the sixty-day folks and they would begin to press. The media would suddenly want more credit info and start talking to whoever was silly enough to spend money with me. My suppliers would ask for cash up front. Clients who had a favorite photographer would ask me to use him or her and I couldn't because I didn't have the cash, couldn't get the credit, and didn't want to ask the client to suddenly start paying up front. Somebody would call from *AdWeek* wanted to know what was happening. Clients would pay for things direct and I'd lose my commissions.

Nobody loves you when.

The pack mentality I'd mentioned was an equally real threat. Things were tough all over Houston and ad budgets are the first to go. When an agency had difficulty, whatever client remained with the shop could expect to be besieged with offers from other agencies, presentations, spec work, lunches that last till Thursday.

There was no good response.

I'd watched it happen a dozen times. The agencies that ultimately pulled out just ignored all the problems, making note of who would ride with them and who wouldn't, and worked like hell to get back into the successful column. Call it momentum or karma or luck, you had to be a winner.

I called Tammy in.

"Pay everything that's less than thirty days," I said.

"But some of them are . . ."

"I know. Pay everything that's less than thirty days and let me know how much is left. Go!"

"The bills aren't even in," she wailed.

"Pay what we've got. I'm trying to confuse the issue."

Then I went to work to collect. Have you ever tried to beg cheerfully? I made jokes through gritted teeth, sympathized with clowns, was respectful to incompetents but tried to collect. To the vague ones, I promised a follow-up call, to people who had blatantly overstepped normal bounds—asking me to fix them up with Margrit—I was humble. I spent the whole afternoon tracking down folks, pathetically few of them, and asking for my money. This was risky but cash talks and so forth.

Some of the suppliers who got a more-than-prompt payment would assume my bookkeeping was screwed up as usual. Others hopefully would talk me up. If *AdWeek* called, I would be positive enough to make your teeth ache. If I had any clients left and they wanted to know how things were going, they couldn't be better. I debated running an agency ad just to spend some visible money and decided against it.

I finished with promises of almost forty thousand within the next few days and I said I'd pick up the checks, which was risky but who wants to mess with the famous check in the mail?

Tammy came in and showed me the checkbook. Six thousand.

"Your next paycheck looks very possible," I said.

"What's happening?" she asked, sitting down and reaching for a cigarette even though she was a violent nonsmoker. "I don't really need this paycheck, the next one's the one I pay rent with." She smiled.

"Don't be silly."

"I mean it."

"I know you do and I can't tell you . . . forget it. I want you to spend the next few days looking around, though."

"Beaumont," she said. "What the hell is happening?"

"I don't know," I said. "But I'm fixing to find out." I picked up the phone, dug out the number, called Ms. Harthorne, and waited for an answer. I started to wave Tammy out and then decided I needed any positive vibes she could waft my way.

The voice repeated the last four numbers and I said, "I would like to speak to Ms. Harthorne, please."

"Your name?"

"Tell her Beaumont's calling."

"One minute."

I waited less than a minute and he came back and said Ms. Harthorne was unavailable. I asked that she call me and he informed me she did not return calls. I said that was rude and he hung up.

I dialed back and asked meekly if I could leave a message. He said, "Don't bother. Ms. Harthorne has a message for you: you missed the deadline."

I hung up first and Tammy looked at me with questions and I said, "We missed the deadline."

"So what," she said, "we always do that."

19

THE PROCESS OF BECOMING BUSTED was a dreary one. I had read the stories about who really ran the city, told a few, listened respectfully in the backs of meeting rooms when the power-people did their thing.

I never knew what it meant.

I didn't flatter myself that I was an important enough fly to deserve the deluxe swatter treatment, no, I was more or less just brushed aside, unable to earn a living because Ms. Harthorne didn't want me to and told somebody to fix it. And me.

They did, thoroughly and completely. I couldn't get a new client to save my soul and in more paranoid moments was convinced "they" were following me around to drive in the spikes. They weren't, of course, they didn't have to. Houston is still a small town in some ways and a quiet word or two was enough, spreading like ripples, touching everybody who might bring a paltry budget my way and let me earn enough bucks to get out from under.

My friends in the agency business were sympathetic but guarded and Tammy was a doll, working without salary at night to help me with the paperwork I couldn't handle, even after she had to leave the payroll. There wasn't a payroll. I wouldn't beg and when I did call Ms. Harthorne I got a curt dismissal from the bored male voice with muscles.

Perhaps I could have scrounged enough marginal work to scratch out an existence but the damn money kept following me around. When I should have been writing, I was in a meeting about my debts or trying to think of a new excuse for an irate caller. My operating credit went first, the simple calling up a supplier to make an assignment. After the first month or so they would be polite, "Gee, I'd like to do this for you but . . ." and they wanted cash and who could blame them? Media people were cruel, calling the ragtag bundle of clients I had left up for payment direct and not even listening to my promises. Without the credit, I lost the float and without the float I couldn't live.

I sold the stat camera which had saved my ass, all but one of the typewriters and everything else I could get my hands on. With the money, a couple of writing assignments, some bones thrown to me by friends, we stayed afloat for two more months, but the handwriting was all over every wall.

The interesting thing was the convergence of every bad factor possible: I finally sold the building under forced-sale circumstances, so I didn't get a very good price for it, so the equity dollars I finally received (mysteriously held up for eleven days by the mortgage company) didn't stave off the creditors long enough for me to get some more work. I didn't eat the American Express lunches anymore since I didn't have a card. Everything was cash for me, the one commodity I didn't have.

I went through the processes of collection: 'Now, I'm sure we can straighten this out . . ." "Your prompt attention . . ." "In order to avoid expensive litigation . . ." I also went through the bad scene with supplier friends who were no longer friends because I couldn't pay them for what they'd done. I got hit too many times and drifted into a catatonic state, barely reacting to gross insults and unable to rouse myself to do anything.

Hector saw me free of charge, which he should have too, the dollars I'd spent on his couch. And told me he couldn't do anything until I made a decision. I told him the decision had been made for me and he said sharply that how I reacted to the circumstances was my decision.

Vince said, "Pack it in."

Tammy said, "We can beat it." But I made her get another job. I disappointed her, I fear, unable to rise to this challenge, unable to beat the odds, I never knew what heroic proportions her mind had made of me.

In the end, I saved the bayhouse and the boats. I put my own house on the market and left, whipped-dog syndrome, heading to the bay with three thousand dollars as my stake, much better than some but with several times that amount hanging over my head, Chapter Seven or not. I owed the money and I would pay it, but when was highly problematical.

It was the first time I'd ever really lost.

Lost, whipped, beaten, destroyed. The words are not so tasty in the mouth, I hated it and the results were as devastating as divorce or a death in the family. I lost all interest in females of any sort, had difficulty focusing for more than a couple of minutes at a time, was subject to a wide variety of strange pains and aches and clutching at the chest. I was glad Margrit was traveling in her new job, wrong about that, too, it appeared, because I couldn't stand to fail her in our bedroom arena and her sympathy would be even worse. I'm sure she found plenty of volunteers to take up the slack.

I didn't even like to fish anymore. What I did mostly was brood about my defeat. I was obsessed by it. In especially bad moments I almost missed the simple and direct way they had attempted to thump my head but then I thought of some of the TV testimony and alleged violence attributed to American Title and decided I should count my blessings.

I was certainly still better off than some folks. That had about as much effect on me as my mother telling me about the starving children in India when I didn't want to eat my peas.

I *was* damn good at getting drunk with Evans, talking late into the night, but he soon got wind of what I was doing and then was always just a little too busy to drink with me.

"I ain't going to watch you fuck yourself," he said bluntly.

The three thousand melted away quickly, college kids need tuition and rent on the dorm and Momma still wouldn't chip in, a tiny aggravation in a fertile field. I tried to write and wrote shit I wouldn't send to magazines and when my agency friend who had backstopped me when I sent Bechman on his nighttime trip into the Gulf sent me some radio spots to do, I missed the deadline twice.

I did a superior job of feeling sorry for myself.

There is a bit of creator's pride—and surprise—in building a business and a mother's loss when it is taken from you. All my life I had believed that all it took was a little more hard work and that is true, I suppose, but I couldn't dig down deep enough to find a solution. It didn't help that the rumors flowed like lava, Beaumont's going under, Beaumont's a hundred forty days behind, Beaumont's losing everything.

I was of course, which makes for good rumors.

Then there's the unintentional cruelty of time. My awards and giant sales successes of a few months ago were old history, credit taken and gone, and my samples looked a little ragged and yellow around the edges. I had not a lot to offer the marginal advertisers who got their awful work done by the media production people and smiled when their abortions hit the papers or blared from the TV. What did they need of style and taste and slick production? Or of me? And what had I done lately?

In a final irony, Bechman's bank paid for its invoices promptly and then switched the account away, so I had been paid for all the hard, low-profit part, the creating and making of the materials, and missed out on the gravy, the commission gained from media, 15 percent for a bit of paper.

The real estate lady, a dragonlike person with a too-loud voice, shouted down the long distance line that I could sell my house tomorrow if I would forget about any profit. I had already done that with the office building. The profit meant my meals and I declined, exhorting her to greater efforts. She wanted me to spend three thousand to rehabilitate, a good investment is what she said, and I pulled out empty pockets and hoped for a miracle.

My income tax took eight hundred on top of the twenty-two thousand I'd had withheld and I'd better not ask for another extension said the accountant who held all my records until I sent him a check for past due work.

Tammy would call and I'd stand in Evans's living room and try to be cheerful numbly and she was making a success of it, working for the private hospital "they might have an advertising budget soon," and I told her they wouldn't give such money to me and to watch out for herself.

The Port Lavaca paper would buy a story now and then, twenty-five bucks and two weeks' waiting and I made a buck here tutoring and there with some "marketing advice," although they never thought they'd got their money's worth since I preached common sense and not a bunch of fancy words.

I would have made it finally, living at idle in a grayish world, if they hadn't tried to kill me. It was probably a zealous bit of enthusiasm, a final solution for the Beaumont question, and it was funny in a way because I was no threat to anyone, they'd brushed the fly away real well, except somebody somewhere in their echelons wanted to make a name for himself, initiative to be rewarded and a ledger entry closed. When chance presented an opportunity, they made the jump.

Vince had told me they were an enormous machine, rolling onward even after the need for rolling had passed, and he must have been right.

I would have made it living at the bay, another piece of flotsam, if they hadn't tried to kill me in the Gulf.

20

T<small>HE</small> T<small>EXAS</small> <small>OFFSHORE FISHING SEA-</small>
son is marked by holidays, Memorial Day to open up and
Labor Day to close. The rest of the time you lick your
wounds and try to get the budget back in balance. Even
doing it yourself as much as possible, an offshore trip in
my boat was a hundred-dollar proposition, more if you
ran through a lot of bait or chased fish a bunch of miles.

At the lower end of the coast, Port Isabel/Padre Island,
it's a bit more like Florida and they fish longer, but for the
bulk of us Memorial Day and Labor Day are the book-
ends.

I woke up realizing I had let the better part of a season
slip me by, eyes firmly buried in my navel and not liking
the field of view. Maybe it was a healthy sign, but I woke
up in the middle of the lonely night and realized I hadn't

burned a thumb against a kingfish or caught my breath to see a sail rising to the baits all year. "So I'm broke, must I be an asshole, too?" I asked Bullit.

I woke up in the morning and spent a day or two of checking and maintenance and launched the boat on a breathless summer evening, big sun teetering on the edge of the western shore, orangy red from the atmospheric dust and beautiful. The bay was glassy, small fish jumped in the slip, and I idled out to catch my bait, not wanting to pay the price for store-bought mullet.

I stalked an oyster reef like the largest heron of them all and correspondingly clumsy when compared to that bird's darting beak. I swirled a nylon cast net at fleeing mullet, judging their size from the tiny wakes they left as they scurried for deeper water. It's a bit like stalking game and fishing and once I had tossed the net over a four-pound redfish and I can't remember which of us was more surprised.

A half hour's work and I had a couple of dozen shiny mullet, six and eight inches, the larger ones gently released to spawn again. They have a characteristic muddy smell, the fertile rich aroma of the marsh which supports the entire food chain, including us. The live well on my boat would keep them fresh and it was dark when I got back to the cabin and I sat inside with a drink and started to feel the first tingle of excitement.

"I think I'm getting well," I said in the dark, and grinned, probably the first real grin in a month.

In the morning I was at the boat well before the false dawn, working by flashlight to check the tanks and tighten down the straps that held batteries secure. I tossed a couple of cans of fuel cleaner in the tanks to mix with condensed water and burn through the carbs. Rods aboard, extra line, steel leaders wrapped the night before after a chili sandwich dinner. Last check on the weather: "two- to four-feet swells, winds from the southeast at

eight to twelve, twenty percent chance of thun-
dershowers . . .'' and I fired up the Yamahas and was the
first boat out, watched by a stray pier cat and two guys
who were too well-dressed for fishing. Tourists.

I set the tachs at 3700 RPM and synched the engines
and an arrow-straight wake peeled out from beneath my
stern and there was just a touch of chill in the air and I
opened a highly improper beer to celebrate. The sun was
coming up over my shoulder and the sea birds were
awake, busy at their demanding task of eating several
times their weight each day.

It would be wrong to say I'd be just as happy in a leaky
rowboat fishing for perch, the expensive craft and equip-
ment are required to get you into the big water where the
excitement is, but I was glad to be at an honest task rather
than coddling a client for dollars. Or the whining, poor,
poor, pitiful me.

A great deal of what I saw and smelled and felt was
original, as-God-made-it, untouched by greasy greedy humans and it was enough to be able to participate in the
natural cycle, though I did it in fiberglass and with gasoline. I was there. There was a hunter's anticipation, too,
why deny it, pitting yourself against an indifferent and
dangerous opponent and a craftsman's pride in doing it
right. The beer was cold and good, and I put the pull tab
in my pocket.

I was breaking several rules, of course. One, of common sense, said I couldn't afford the gasoline. Another
mandated that you never go offshore alone, falling overboard and watching the boat disappear over the horizon
always a possibility. Finally, no one knew my plans for
the day and correspondingly no one would begin a search
if I had trouble, emergency Channel 16 on the radio,
Coast Guard choppers circling, private boats alerted to
look for a twenty-five-foot Grady-White and a six-foot-
two fool.

Blue-green water was close to the beach, maybe two miles after I went through the roller coaster ride at the mouth of the jetties, taking care to avoid shoal water to port. I found an interesting-looking weed line, filled with trash and debris, wondering how one leather shoe found its way there, bottles, plastic, the remains of a wooden pallet, and complex seaweed.

I worked the weed line south, ocean debris brought together in a straggly line to the horizon, weaving in and out its edges. When we got the water filled up with trash, we were through, I thought. But in the meantime, it made a natural fish haven and I trolled lures tipped with mullet, toward the spot where I had abandoned poor Bechman and I thought of him briefly and supposed he had found another bank to terrify or was he like some others I had known, autocratic despots suddenly stripped of power and finding it tough sledding—pathetic really, how they couldn't find another role to play without the backup perks and awe.

I had opened the second beer when the first fish hit and the reel screeched an unholy, happy sound and the beer went spewing across the deck and I chopped the throttles and felt the unmistakable heart-stopping rush of an angry kingfish, king mackerel, a streamlined torpedo of a fish, no swim bladder to let him float, so swimming endlessly from moment of birth with lean muscles generating incredible power against the pull of my monofilament line. He came to gaff and I dropped the ugly steel hook, not wishing to stab him for what he was born to do, and pulled him aboard by the leader, avoiding sharp teeth flopping. One giant eye stared at me without fear, fair fight and the odds were on his side, twenty pounds against two hundred, and I lifted him overboard, sinking in the depths for a second before he shot away. I retrieved my beer and found it salty.

I worked my weed line for the morning, keeping only a

tasty dolphin, dorado fish, for supper and enjoyed the loneliness, away from the cluttered oil rigs and fin-tailed boats which made me shake my head. They'd probably put more poundage aboard, beer bellies swaying in the sun and rough voices cursing when you trolled through their chum lines, a social activity really, and I wanted none of it.

You tire easily in the Gulf, boat chores, lures to be cleaned, the struggle with the fish, and I was through by early afternoon, ravenous and sunburned and feeling good. I drifted the debris a bit, nosing the boat within it and cutting off the engines with that faint scary feeling—will they start?—and there was not another human in sight, the only sign of our occupancy of this planet a distant rig in the horizon's haze. I watched small shiny fish glints in the trash, a whole world here, with an occasional predator coming to feed, predator like me but for better reasons.

The engines started fine of course and I eased the boat toward the jetties, seeing a black dot coming out of the sun toward me, and it was a Bertram, that classic thirty-one-foot hull which set a new standard for offshore craft, tuna tower and riggers bouncing in the swell, he was hard on it, pushing the boat more than needed, some of the Bertrams will run over forty with a tune-up and a clean bottom and you're welcome to the fuel bills, although the boat is an old friend of a dream.

I altered course a notch to give him sea room, admiring the hull as he pounded on, and the bow lined up on me like a gunsight. I changed course again, annoyed, it's a big ocean out here why play chicken, and it became obvious that I was his goal.

So I pulled the throttles back and idled in a circle, watching him approach over my shoulder when I was pointed away from him, was this idiot ever going to slow down? The bow abruptly settled and threw a wake and he expertly used his momentum to come about in a neat half-turn and lay beside me, looking down from the larger boat, two men in the cockpit holding glasses, I hate glass containers on a boat. Pinkish white dead skin, brand-new caps, dark glasses. The guy on the bridge was dark-tanned unlike his sports, who reminded me, who might have been, my early-morning observers back at the dock.

Was it directions or fishing information or just a beery good companionship? I didn't care, I just wanted him gone from my patch of ocean and I nodded to the tower and the man at the controls and waited.

"Hey! How's it going, sport?" From the cockpit and I faked a smile and told them it was okay, an odd meeting this in the Gulf, we usually gave each other a bit of elbow room, what did they want, to chat?

"I got a couple. If it's kingfish, they're hitting yellow with a trailer hook and this weed line is good. Farther out if you want to try for a sail, although I haven't heard of any. The shrimpers are back north, out from the jetties." Fishing report from Beaumont, now go away please.

The skipper reversed, just touching his throttles, and brought the stern of the Bertram to my boat's side, too close, and I grabbed my throttles to jump out of his way, but he killed the thrust and one of the guys in the cockpit, where were their rods, looked at me and asked, "Are you Beaumont, by any chance?"

I must have started and he looked at my left hand, two fingers not there and no time to hide that fact, and he nodded. Before I had a chance to say anything, he swung his legs over the Bertram's stern to jump aboard and say hello. I started forward instantly, repel boarders, and thought better of it, mind working at maximum efficiency, concentration seeing each movement he made as an individual segment, weight on his left hand *here*, pivot *there*, leading foot approaching my gunwhale *now*, right hand stretching out *so*.

I slammed both throttles back and the engines kicked into reverse with a roar and my stern dipped away from his approaching foot and I saw the muscles in his supporting arm lock as he sought to contain his inertia and I was moving away, roaring engines muted as their torque pulled the stern down, water washing across my bare feet from the transom.

The Bertram's skipper saw my move and duplicated it, his bigger screws giving him an acceleration lead, even with the broad beam he had to pull through the water, and fiberglass screeched with a horrid sound as the heavier boat smashed into mine obliquely and I put the wheel over hard to get away from the noise, the boarder now perched on his gunwhale ready to leap and my bow was clear. I shifted without waiting for the RPMs to die down and hoped the Japanese designers had over-engineered the shifting forks.

It was Miami-to-Nassau racing there for a minute, but I had a couple of tons less weight and pulled ahead. The wind became a factor quickly because I had a speed advantage of six or eight miles an hour but he could cut through the swells, superior hull and thrust of weight, if I backed off the throttles even a touch. I caught a glimpse of someone clambering up the ladder to the tower, with a stick, and suddenly realized the stick was probably a 30.06 caliber stick and pounded the heel of my hand against wide open throttles. How high were the wind and the corresponding waves? In the open Gulf I could outrun him but the margin wasn't large because I couldn't hold the engines wide open and stay inside the boat, stainless grip rails or not.

We leaped from wave to wave and I feared burying the bow and turning two tons of boat upside down on top of me. Every time the props came clear, the tachs swung around against the stop and rods were clattering on the deck, the gaff lodged against the transom, sliding Plexiglas doors to the radio compartment swinging back and forth crazily, big ice chest smashed against the side of the boat and spilling beer cans and ice everywhere. I pulled the engines back a notch to no appreciable difference in the wild ride and tried to judge the distance to my pursuer, was he gaining? I tried another notch and the speed-ometer sensor, the Pitot tube, on the transom must have broken off because the needle abruptly swung from close to fifty to zero and I was gaining on him, I could see it now. My port engine picked this time to sputter and the tachometer dipped and the boat started easing to the left. I didn't know what caused it, didn't those Japs allow for eight thousand revs when the props came clear? I nursed the throttle back and forth and it sputtered again and I had to apply steering pressure to keep us running true, the Bertram now perhaps a half mile back and more than a dozen miles to civilization and comforting other boats as witnesses.

I would have paid dearly for a new set of plugs and maybe a whole tune-up then, bring me a riding engineer when people in fancy boats are trying to kill me. For I had not the slightest doubt that that was their aim, my stom-ach clenching and bruised arms tight on the wheel.

I could hold just over 4500 RPM on the port engine and matched that on the other and the boat rode a bit easier now and I judged I could hold my lead through the jetties but not across the expanse of bay between me and Port O'Connor. It was that close or maybe closer because the Bertram looked like it was gaining now and I tried full throttle on the port engine and got sputtering, boat lurch-ing. They'd get me just inside the jetties, near as I could tell.

The stick guy was pointing his weapon at me and I wished him all the best, because at our speed even the heavy Bertram would be shaking and bouncing and leaping and if he hit me, it would be God's will sure enough, so take your best shot, fella, bring a shotgun next time.

The tachs drifted a touch lower even though I had not moved the throttles and the Bertram was gaining now, you could see it, and I caught a momentary flash of white, spray from the waves against the jetty's end dead off my bow. I'd be there a minute or more and they'd be hard on my stern.

What would they do? A rifle shot is okay in the Gulf where they could weigh the body and have an excellent chance of never hearing a word about it. But if they planned on an abandoned boat scenario, they'd have to explain the damage to my hull. Or maybe that would fit. If I had to kill me, I thought, I'd just run over the boat, surely the Bertram could take it, they build those things like a tank. But they need to do that in open water, the bay's not deep enough to hide the wreck or spill of oil and greasy gas. So it would be a rifle shot, get close enough and you wouldn't miss even in a bouncing boat, and the bay chop, abrupt and close together, would slow them less than I.

They could tow me out for a proper burial.

I would have made a pretty picture, great ad for Grady-White, when I came across the cross chop at the mouth of the jetties. The boat flew through the air, four thousand pounds airborne, engines screaming, and crashed bow down in the next roller and solid green water came across the bow and swept everything back to the stern and the Bertram gained another hundred yards. I caught a glimpse of a solitary fisherman locked against the jetty rocks, mouth open, what's the matter, buddy, never seen a boat fly before?

We pounded through the twin granite arms at all the speed I could muster and they were grinning back there now, confident they'd have me just about the time we came into the bay. I couldn't make the engines run any faster and my legs were aching where they'd smashed against the console, despite my grip on the wheel.

I gained the hundred yards back with a desperate swerve to the right as soon as we came into the bay, right not left toward Port O'Connor and that fooled them and I gained but the damn engines were slowing even more now, lousy plugs misfiring, and I took the only chance I could see.

Jetties change the natural balance between sand and water and after a time an enormous sand flat, shoal water for sure, had built up at the base of the north jetty. It didn't show on the charts and we didn't have time for charts, so I picked what looked like a likely stretch and held the boat there at an estimated forty per. I watched the wake, pretending I was staring at the bigger boat behind, looking for a tiny trail of sand kicked up by the roaring props.

I wanted just the tips, the very bottom parts of my engines, the skegs, to be touching, kicking up the sand.

It was a matter of mechanics, physics, displacement, Archimedes would have been proud of me. The Bertram props were almost three feet down, even on plane at speed, and my boat required less than half of that. Outboards versus inboards, four thousand pounds versus eight. I screamed across the flat, arcing in a huge half-circle to keep that trail of sand behind, and the Bertram slid up on the flat, dug in the props, and smashed to a rotten halt with an anguished roar, sand and water spraying everywhere. Probably the hull would never be quite right again, too many forces unleashed against it.

Their engines roared for several seconds until somebody cut the switches, beautiful boat tilted at a crazy angle.

I hoped they smashed their faces against all sharp objects and hard surfaces aboard that they could find and I was tempted to circle and wave in triumph but decided against it because I had to edge my way off the shoal and keep the boat on plane. I'd never get it off if I slowed and sunk down in the water.

I got off it, the Bertram receding in the distance, no small figures examining the damage visible, maybe they were all knocked cold or worse. I pulled back to just barely planing and headed for Point Lookout.

I felt better than I'd felt in months, adrenaline slowly draining, but alive, really alive, and the air had never smelled sweeter and I applauded diving herring gulls and laughed at jumping mullet.

The boat ran sweetly at this lower speed and I lashed the wheel and went back and found that the speed-ometer's Pitot tube had just popped loose so I could put it in place and I could see my speed again. Rather more conservative now.

I stowed the rods, straightened up the ice chest, picked up the beer, edged the throttles up, and headed for home.

I had gone quietly. Even politely. You'd figure they would have let well enough alone.

21

I WAS STILL RIDING A HIGH WHEN I swooped into the slip, throwing far too much wake, they'd forgive me this once. I made short work of getting the boat on the trailer and hauled it the half mile to the house, did a record washdown and stored the rods, locked up, told Evans I had an appointment back in town and left.

"Looks like something important, good luck," he said.

"I . . . thank you," I said, and was on my way.

It was just plain stupid, that was all, stupid and I was grateful for it. What I suspect happened is that some half-brain figured he had a chance to make his mark, decisive and strong and sudden, and only I would be against it. Why else make an attempt under circumstances that were less than perfect?

Probably somebody got to the "Initiative" section of *The Hoodlum's Manual*, something like that. It was dumb.

I had learned my lesson, I knew my place, but they left me with nothing to lose. After years of being snoopy, I called it an active curiosity, my transgression long ago in poor Tuckerman's office seemed a lifelong burden. But I felt good, reasons for the vendetta forgotten and buried but the action still live and my senses alert. Hell, I wished they would have chased me weeks ago, Bertram drivers whipped and stuck. The original Xerox of those transactions was lost in my move, to boot. Who cared?

So I steered the car down to Houston, sixty-seven on cruise control, one quick stop at the Palacios bank to withdraw the rest of my capital, thirteen hundred and they didn't want to give it to me, much checking of ID and muttering between bank officers and a grudging teller. I took hundreds mostly and smiled my way out. I was off with my war chest and an especially cold Lite beer, wondering when I'd be back and would the kingfish wait?

I hit the Southwest Ramada again and decided against it because I'd stayed there before and the Bertram would get pulled off and they'd check the bay and see that I was gone and maybe they knew I'd stayed there before. Besides, the desk clerk didn't like my cash and I had a long memory. So I found an off-brand, I liked their sign, and made a deal for a week and they seemed grateful for the money, a nice touch that.

Houston in many ways is a staggering city, gleaming buildings looming on several widely separated horizons and a mass of people scurrying, but the traffic wasn't as bad as I remembered it and there were For Lease signs everywhere, the oil depression hitting hard. I was sorry, for I loved the tasteless, damn-the-torpedoes energy of the place and hoped it would come back soon.

I didn't have a plan but I was bursting with energy,

half-formed thoughts spilling from my brain, and I bought a bottle of good bourbon, hit the ice machine, and slipped off my shoes before I made the first call.

"Who's your favorite old advertising guy?" I asked.

"Beaumont!"

"How you doing, kid?"

"Great, everything's great. Where are you?" There was joy in her hurried words and I looked at the phone a little surprised, I'd have thought the affection would be dimmed by now but I didn't feel like talking too much, a thousand spy stories stirring my memory.

"I'm around. What time do you get off?"

"About thirty minutes, damn I'm glad to hear you, your voice, I mean, I'm glad you called!"

"Remember where we used to have a drink after work?"

"Sure," she said. "At the—"

"Don't say it, but why don't you drive by there after work, okay?"

"I'll leave now, but what—"

"Hey. Humor me," I interrupted.

"Of course. I'll leave here now. Fifteen minutes?"

"Yeah, but just drive by. Don't go in the parking lot."

A silence then, had I lost my marbles? And she said sure and she would leave as soon as she straightened up her desk, she had lots to tell me, was I back for good?

"For bad, I hope," I said, and said good-bye. I finished my drink and went back to the car and hoped Evans was taking good care of Bullit. I'd left her sniffing around the cats he kept, to kill the snakes in country wisdom, and hoped she'd find détente with them. Probably the cats could kick her butt, sissy city dog.

I was in position across the street when Tammy drove by, one more pretty girl behind the wheel of a sporty car she couldn't afford, but I was in no position to lecture. I watched for following cars, saw none or none that I could recognize and speeded up to catch her at the Loop and Westheimer, honked and waved. She finally saw me and jumped, her foot slipping off the brake, and in her waving she idled forward and bumped the car ahead of her, the driver giving her a disgusted look. She hit him with the fifty-watt smile and he melted, no harm done. We rendezvoused in the Galleria parking lot and she came running from the hatchback, jumping on me with enthusiasm, skirt swirling wildly, and kissed me hard.

How have you been, what's the reason for the visit, are we going to go back in business, they've forgotten us now and let's go have dinner, good to see you, kissing again.

I untangled myself and suggested drinks at the top of one of the Galleria's two hotels and we parked and went there, bourbon on the rocks and gimlet.

"Gimlet, you're changing from the beer-girl."

"Do you think it makes me look mature?" Eyelashes quite long, I'd never noticed that, firm young body, blonde spikes gone in favor of what I call a pixie cut, I'm sure it's the wrong nomenclature, I can't keep up.

"Love the hair," I said. "It appeals to the hidden homosexual in me."

"My last illusion . . . shattered," she said dramatically, and threw her arms across her eyes, bringing nipples hard against the sheerness of the blouse even through the bra, and I looked away.

She told me about her job, increasing responsibilities, file clerks and typists to supervise, two raises in four months, "but one was after the trial basis, so it doesn't count," missing the agency business, "the people are so straight," no new Boyfriend but a plentitude of boyfriends, she said, making the initial cap with her voice, and I was unreasonably jealous and frightened for her, a parent's vague fears.

I told her what had happened, brushing aside some of the lonely lostness of my stay at the bay and making the

Bertram's threat perhaps less than it was, my role remaining the same, beefed up a bit.

She was a joy, as always, picking up the nuance from my voice, face mirroring the emotions I described, confiding too much, no employer barriers now, how old was she.

"I'm twenty-six," she said, "you missed my birthday and I want a kiss." And got it too, tongue darting suddenly, I didn't know what or how to respond and I was flustered then, suddenly not a father at all but couldn't take advantage, hero worship, down and out, all that love and sympathy and sheer goodness bursting out, and flowing over me and I started to weep.

"Jesus Christ!" I said.

"Most men respond somewhat differently," she said deadpan, and we laughed at that, tears splattering into the bourbon and I told her about the first kingfish and the salty beer.

"I want to go down there with you," she said, looking straight at me. "I've got a week after November."

Dinner then, no store-bought, waiter-served meal would do, but she had to cook for me and did, her chicken not quite up to Margrit's standard, but I'd never tell. I had to call Margrit.

We didn't talk about my plans because I had none, really, just an unformed realization that I had to win, and when the evening came too close to something else entirely, I excused myself, pleading extreme fatigue and made a joke about being old. She kissed me good-night at the door with a force that left me walking awkwardly until I got control.

I drove to the motel quietly, through empty spotlighted streets, and wondered just how much of a bastard could I be.

Couldn't sleep and at thirty minutes past midnight, I drove to Vince's and walked around to the alley entrance and pounded on the big steel door until he came to answer, keeping away from the backlit entrance until he was sure it was me. And he hugged me briefly and gave me drinks in his office "unless you just have to watch a girl undress" and I was glad to see him, more than I could say.

The girl who brought us drinks wore jeans and a man's shirt, no bra, and I ached and drank and ached.

Closing time and I was stumbling, Vince wouldn't let me drive. I didn't argue too much and asked for a cab and got Saki, who took me to her apartment, giggling at my profound stupidities and polysyllable humor. She undressed me there, tiny Oriental hands busy exploring, and I don't remember much but I was a riot, that seems accurate.

I WOKE UP WITH A FORCE TEN HANG-over, watery spots swimming upward across my field of vision, shaking hands, the raw taste of bile in my mouth, and Saki asleep like an angel. I cursed faintly when there was no cold beer to be had and stumbled into my clothes. Out the door, unfamiliar neighborhood, an icehouse down the block, thank God. After I had choked and sputtered, I finished off the first can and asked for another, barman eyeing me without respect, drunks not welcome here.

I found I had enough money for a cab and reclaimed my car, the sensible Chevy parked close to Vince's door, where it would be in the lights. No 'Vette anymore, a forced swap at the Port Lavaca used car lot, six hundred cash in greasy bills for boot, I had missed my car immediately. I drove to my friendly motel, with one quick stop to send flowers to Saki, an unexpected treat I hope and thankful she was listed, it would have been hard to explain to Vince why I needed her address and I doubt he sent flowers even to a nightingale.

Motel showers are a gift and I used mine well and thought that with a little food I could face the day. What to do was, of course, the question. My early conquest of Bechman didn't seem quite such a coup right now and I doubted I could repeat that scenario, so what was I to do?

They had taken away my business. Maybe I could have found a way to fight harder or go to work for someone else. But my troubles might come along with me, an albatross hung firmly around my neck, and who would wish that on a friend? I had retreated to the bay and I was happy enough there, idling engines can run forever, but they had tried to kill me in the Gulf. No place was safe and I didn't want to die and as Ms. Harthorne had said, I had no options.

"It's me or them," I said to the shower walls, and laughed at my own drama. A man who can laugh at himself can't be all bad, I reassured the voice inside that constantly put me down. I didn't plan an Eastwood blazing forth in righteous gunfire for I lacked the necessary skills and courage. But communications was my business, my trade, the only thing I knew and my best bet. It would make life interesting enough, trying, and I had no options. I'd like to force the bitch out of her aloof calm, separate her from the hulk, and rip the superiority from her face.

I had about twelve hundred fifty bucks and twenty years' experience and I was highly motivated.

"They'd better watch their ass," I said to the towel, and giggled.

I felt almost human and a greasy-good cheeseburger finished off the rehabilitation. All I needed was a plan.

I went to the library and registered for a card, persuaded a nice lady to show me how to work the microfilm and went looking among newspaper files for what the public knew about ATIG. There was a surprising amount of stuff on file, reporters' innuendos carefully stated, names of companies and people, and I was meticulous in my list making. When they closed and kicked me out I had a better picture of their operations, which seemed to be divided into those that made money and those that did something with it. Bars and video games, an escort service, pawnshops, siding outfits, odd construction companies were among the former. Then they controlled some consumer finance companies, a mortgage banker, and an S&L. Bechman's bank was nowhere connected, in print.

I called an old acquaintance, a reporter on the defunct *Houston Press* and then the evening paper, whom I had met when he made a valiant effort to get some easy PR money and found the work not to his liking. I used to laugh at him, struggling with reporters' ethics and PR needs. But out of my appreciation for this moral battle, some sort of minor friendship had grown, helped along by our mutual fondness for whiskey and chasing girls. We talked a lot and I remember little action. We drank a great deal better.

"I thought you'd died and gone to hell," he said over the phone, and I assured him I was alive and well and offered to buy him a late dinner. But no, he was married again and she had two kids, he loved the kids he said unabashedly, and he was staying home these nights, back working for the newspaper again. Why didn't I drop by?

I would and did and he had gone the full route, suburban tract home, 3-2-2 with detached garage/workroom and that was where we met, after I had inspected the kids and said hello to a wary young wife, dark eyes hidden behind long dark sixties hair.

"She looks very sweet," I said, nursing a beer.

"She's changed my life and it's boring but I love it," he

said. "What brings you here after, what, three years?" He was almost a caricature of a stage Irishman, down to the red veins in his face, broad flat planes dusted with freckles, thinning hair cut very short, and a husky, knowing voice.

"I'm interested in a company called American Title Investment Group," I said.

"Why?"

"Do you know them?"

"What I read, only."

"That's it?"

"I know what everybody knows, they're some sort of holding company with a faintly bad odor."

"Did you know they controlled one of the biggest banks around?" And I gave him parts, bits, and pieces of the Bechman story and looked for a reaction.

He shrugged, "So far, so what?"

"It's a story surely."

"Come on, Beaumont, you're supposed to be a pro," he said angrily, and got another beer for himself without asking me.

"What's that mean?"

"That means there's no story here, nothing you can support, nothing that an editor is gonna take and run with, no facts, just an audiotape, nonadmissible, duress, no independent verification, no real crime that I can see, nothing you can get on and ride."

I started to protest and he held up a silencing hand, still angry, possibly affronted that his breed was powerless.

"I'm out of that, in management, even have some input into sales," he said.

"And you say things like 'input' now," I said into a silence.

"Yes, I do, and what of it!" We drank beer a while and I asked about the kids he'd inherited and he brightened at once and told me their wondrous tales, much like my wondrous tales or anyone's. And he was a bit abashed, some old instincts still prodding his comfortable life, and plainly wished I hadn't come. I felt like I was far from my place and excused myself, tell your wife I was glad to meet her, and started to leave, knowing I'd not be back.

"Get a story. Or something that looks like a story and we'll run with it," he said. "We have to or the competition will. But it's got to be a real story." He sat in his garage and waved a good-bye and I let myself out, catching just a glimpse of his wife in a sheer nightgown heading from the inner sanctum as I left and I hoped he would be comforted by her and wished them both well.

A story, huh? Inside of every advertising person there burns a fantasy to be a legitimate reporter or a producer, great films, massive exposés, headlines, awe, documentary film festivals, newsreels. I'd give him a story, hell, I'd package it up and do the final cut. The only problem was I didn't know where it started or where it would end, but that shouldn't stop somebody accustomed to making up important benefits to sell things. Any things, anybody with ad money.

I went back to the motel and called Margrit at the Warwick, ignoring two messages from Tammy for "Mr. Bart." I liked the pseudonym, liked its tough sound.

23

W<small>ONDER OF WONDERS, I GOT HER</small>
on the phone. Without giving my own name, a successful
circumventing of a vigilant private secretary, male, who
sounded remarkably like a movie star, tough roles, hard-
edged words beneath politeness.

"Don't say my name," I said, wondering if they taped
the calls into the suite. "Can you meet me someplace?"

"Of course," she said, "I'll see you at the Y."

Margrit had a supple body far removed from need of
aerobics chanted by a serious instructor and I had no idea
which YMCA she meant. Or maybe YWCA. I asked where
and what but she had abruptly hung up so I leaped downstairs and got the car and headed in on the Southwest
Freeway, Greenbriar exit over by Rice University, and cir-
cled the Warwick fountain, happily free of the detergent

people used to toss among the spraying nozzles to make a street of bubbles.

It worked, because I caught her exiting the Warwick parking garage, no rusty VW these days but a conservative black BMW, ah, how things had changed. When I drew alongside and waved, she ignored me, did a take and wheeled into the parking lot, got out and came over, extended hand, everybody's got a new hairdo, this one severe but she could still make me walk into a wall.

"It is good to see you," she said serenely.

"And you," I said, reading lines.

We agreed upon a bar, an unmarked door in the River Oaks shopping center, dark and quiet and filled with grappling couples upstairs. She ordered a glass of wine and settled back to look up at me, commenting that I'd lost a little weight. I'd lost more, but kept quiet. She was wearing a wedding ring.

"Your new job seems to be working out okay," I said. "The BMW yours?"

"It's one of the ones I use," she said.

I had a quick sense of loss, not of Margrit because I never really had her, only borrowed. But she was so . . . serene is the word that comes to mind, I felt a sense of loss for myself. Everybody had a place, even wild and crazy Margrit, and the world was somewhat dimmer without her frantic thrashing and gyrations, her implausible schemes and reckless efforts.

We don't want the moths to stop fluttering.

Where did I go wrong? I should have accepted the game instead of playing off, by myself mostly, on a tangential course. It was too late now, of course, with habits ingrained and rationalizations embedded, but I felt a sense of loss, a tiny nagging fear that I'd *never* rest easy in the brain, never content to take the established route and my companions would drop away one by one, ex-drinking buddies with two proud kids and weird Margrit in tailored suit still sipping the first glass of wine.

Her job was working out, she'd taken over and begun to "impact" several of the established routines, show the way to more efficiencies, clear up some knotty problems. Ms. Harthorne had come to rely more and more on her in judgmental matters and she enjoyed the consequent rewards, delicate negotiations and careful handling of special clients and blind carbon copies, "personal and confidential," and I was lost and angry, wanting to tear her down or bring her back to some sort of reality, you pick.

"Do you do clients or just the Lady Boss?" I asked crudely.

She slipped that gracefully and changed the subject back to me and all the guards came up, my love in the enemy's camp and enjoying it, and soon we were chatting carefully, guarded, watch your words and plant a seed of misdirection, a careful magician hard at work.

The drinks went into dinner, served by the same solicitous waiter who refilled my glass and admirably kept us supplied with clean ashtrays. Her tastes had changed. She handled the menu French nicely and ate little and I, surly, ordered a steak and fries, "bloody." She was still on the same blasted glass of wine and I finally finished a too-rare piece of meat, reached out and dumped it in the water tumbler. Goddamn, they hadn't given her a brain transplant, somewhere behind this façade was wild and crazy Margrit.

She looked down modestly at her plate for what seemed a long time and the waiter came to clear, catching quick looks at me, would I make a scene, between his errands. I reached out and took her hand, fingertips on the palm, and ordered coffee and Bailey's without a consultation and when it was served she finally looked up and welcome back.

"You got some place where we can go?" she asked.

Waiter happy now, fights all gone, tipping far too much but he should be rewarded for his haste, knows when things are urgent and important, wise man.

Back to my motel and drive on past and register at another, a last-minute caution even though she had her hand lightly on me from the moment we reached the car. Two motels, what the hell I'm rich and I need it, and she was lovely in amber light filtering through heavy motel curtains.

It wasn't love, perhaps, but no secrets between us, a body honesty which is more than most and a special sort of primitive communication, which made everything else go away. But she was up and dressed too quickly, consulting a watch, she never wore a watch, and I lay there naked on the bed and wondered. Be neat if we could stay on a sexual plateau of excitement and anticipation on a continual basis, wouldn't it?

"I haven't got much time," she said tentatively.

"It'll take me a bit to recuperate," I said.

"Not that—you haven't lost your touch, have you?— but I've got to be back on time."

"Your job seems . . ."

"It's not that."

"Then . . ."

"It's more than a job," she said, lighting her first cigarette.

"Tell me."

"Lois . . . likes me." I granted her that with a wave, on to more important things, mind tangled in fetid visions. "But I can't exactly take off an afternoon. Or an evening."

"Is this an occupation or white slavery?" I asked, and stole a cigarette.

"It's a profession, but they're very demanding."

Demanding wasn't the word, a generous portion of her salary "invested" every month, good things, cars, the watch, clothes, but there every minute and departures discouraged. Nothing to complain to the cops about, every benefit there on paper, but no freedom. Or the perception of no freedom, which is the same. I didn't ask about the ring, maybe she got the wrong finger.

"Do you want out?" I asked.

"I don't know. I've *never* been able to live like this."

"And how do you find it?"

"I like it. I really do."

"But the conditions outweigh the benefits?" I asked while jumping into my pants and shirt, if a serious conversation is required dress for it, wish I had a bottle.

"I don't know. They're strange."

"Strange?"

"The mix of people. Some of them make me shiver and Lois is so nice," And tasty, too, I'll bet but don't say it, this is as close as I'll get to the enemy camp.

I lifted an eyebrow and waited.

And I got fifteen minutes' worth, impressions, words, a name or two, quick nervous smiles for punctuation, and I think I'd never loved her more and it wasn't enough, I was taking information as well as love and in bleakness asked the questions, knowing it wasn't going to be.

Back to her car at the nameless bar, quick smile and peck and glance around to see who's looking, and she was gone and I knew she'd not be back, already jeopardizing all she'd ever wanted. And she found it lacking, I bled for her a little.

But I knew more now, Margrit and the library, information is power, right? She had paid a price for a luxury life and I probably shouldn't have busted back into her vision. But I needed what she knew and what did that make me?

24

W<small>HAT</small> I <small>HAD IN MIND WAS COM</small>-parable to taking over General Motors, with twelve hundred fifty dollars as my capital. This particular octopus was huge, disguised, tricky, very probably smarter than I and certainly more ruthless.

It was money and organization, and I'd had a taste of what that meant in a minor key. Get what you need, cars of boats or planes or three thugs to pound a head, and handle the expense later without thought, routine.

Is it any wonder I spent three days doing nothing?

I talked to Tammy, of course, but avoided her invitations because I wasn't quite sure what was appropriate. I knew what my body wanted, her nipples pressing against the sheer blouse a vivid memory, but a nagging conscience kept me from doing anything. Her blatant gestures could be strictly friendly, she was my daughter's buddy and far younger than I. Still, she was undeniably gorgeous and she thought me wonderful.

Margrit was not available by phone and the secretary very insistent on getting my name the single time I called. I logged hours of daytime TV, sneaked into Vince's, made dozens of lists and plans, and vegetated. I would have gone back to the bay except I felt safer here and they took my second week's rent as if I were a very valuable customer, indeed. At current rates, I was good for about seven weeks, I calculated, and then I had to make some money, do something even if it was wrong.

Vince offered to send me to bartender school.

Saki loved the flowers and we were best buddies, no colored-water drinks allowed, and I couldn't sit with her too long without seriously harming her income. I tried to explain but she was having none of it and Vince grinned at my plight before warning me not to hurt her.

I thought of printing a brochure and nailing it to the church door but I couldn't decide which church and I didn't have the money for the printing. Who'd believe me? Bechman's tape was a start and I still had the cassette but I couldn't think of a single way to get it into any usable form.

In the end, mostly to be doing something, I rented a video camera outfit, portable VHS, and decided to tape a day in the life of Ms. Harthorne. Maybe the tape and a few license numbers might be a place to start. I went back to Vince's and arranged to borrow the trusty van again, played with the outfit in the afternoon as the girls were coming in and even taped a few, dancing for the camera.

Their dance interpretations were considerably more liberal in private, no pasties required, and the low light levels gave the tape a surreal quality. Every movement trailed a colored swoop of light. They were all blurred and fuzzy, and when we played it back slow motion they were erotic in a way the sweaty flesh never really is. They were impressed and I gave them the tape for Vince to play on the big-screen TV which had been reserved for Oiler football.

"Ort," I said. "Poetry in motion, real ort."

He and I had a serious talk and I explained what I had in mind, sounding silly in my ears. He thought and could not devise a better plan, feeling that I was spinning wheels yet all too aware I could be dead without luck and an instinctive wariness.

"You're sure they were going to kill you?" he asked.

"You just don't do that, come aboard another guy's boat, there's no reason for it. Besides, they had a gun."

"Beaumont," he said. "How do you manage to get tangled up like this?"

His alternative, finally, was to use Margrit to get to the Boss Lady and do some dreadful and unspecified things to her, an escalation like the Libyan raid, yet she had all the planes. I had no stomach for it, preferring to try the third-party route.

"I feel more comfortable with cameras than guns, anyway."

He just shrugged and asked when I would bring Tammy by. For which I had no answer and that alone stung me into calling her and asking her out for dinner.

Four hours later I decided she'd be the perfect woman for me with ten more years under her belt and told her so. On impulse, dictated perhaps by finances, I took her to Houston's oldest and by no means finest Mexican restaurant, a once-proud chain now shrunk to two, with genuine adobe walls sagging under endless coats of paint. The food was peculiar and I loved it, cooked in steamy vats with decades of savory buildup or at least that's the way I visualized it, never having had the courage to peek in the kitchen. Boy, it was good. Where other ladies had pushed and picked and complained, Tammy dug in, crunching through the finest enchiladas made by man, asking for more tostadas, letting the chili con queso grease drip where it may.

She had the good taste to comment on the perfect service, gray-headed Mexican men secure in their dignity and years, and the spotless starched white tablecloths and heavy china.

"I'll be sorry later," I said. "But it was worth it."

"I won't and I'm glad we came here. Have you been coming long?"

"Since about the time you were born," I said in dismay, and she made a mouth and crunched her taco with such enthusiasm I could hear it across the table. Another margarita, *por favor*.

"How do you feel about naked girls?" I asked.

"I see one every morning."

"Professionals, dancers, at a club I go to."

"Beaumont," she said. "Are you trying to corrupt a minor?"

"I don't know *what* I'm doing and that's the truth," I said. "But I do hang out at one of the topless clubs, the owner's a friend and I feel safe there. And you're twenty-six."

We went and she registered about a nine-point-five on the Vince scale, which is an achievement in anybody's book. I had once asked him if the continual exposure to gorgeous young ladies with few clothes had dulled his appetites and he confessed to a hankering for panty girdles and that was as much as I knew of his love life.

But Tammy made a hit. Even the girls liked her, with the exception of poor Saki, who I heard mutter something about "Merican cows" and who sat off in the corner all night. We continued on the margaritas and everything took on a lovely glow and they insisted on showing Tammy *Beaumont's Movie* after the last customer had been ejected.

We went home in an expensive cab and I declined a

nightcap invitation and she looked at me strangely and went inside, I wonder if I was playing too hard to get.

The next morning I had a thirst like a camel and I stopped on the way to surveillance to pick up a gallon jug of drinking water which I packed in ice.

I learned several things in my first day's work. One is that it's hard to continue surveilling if you constantly have to find a place to relieve your bladder, no more drinking water. The other is that it's the most mind-boggling boring thing that has yet been devised to put a man to sleep.

No sign of Ms. Harthorne, her outsized body-guard/driver, dear Margrit, or even No-Neck and Court. I speculated if they'd really quit and decided not. I was positioned behind the blacked-out windows of the van, camera at the ready, draining the battery from a cigarette lighter attachment. God, it was boring. I lasted till about three that day and packed it in, convinced that I was five kinds of a fool.

Margrit showed up the next morning about ten and told a bunch of stuff to the garage attendant and I wished for a shotgun mike so I could get some idea of what was going on. I dutifully taped her although it was hardly in-criminating. Ms. Harthorne's limo didn't show and I didn't tail Margrit.

"That's the 'action' so far," I told Vince, who wanted to go fishing. I offered him the cabin at Point Lookout and he said he didn't want to take my boat. We argued about that for a time, hell, he could use the nearly indestructible little boat, for that matter, but he was having none of it. I suddenly realized he was a touch uneasy about the water and knots and ropes and seamanship and I was tickled to be one up.

"Let me try this taping stuff another day and I'll take you," I said. "You have to protect me from the bad guys."

He nodded somberly.

But the next day I finally got some interesting tape and a busted head, in that order.

25

MARGRIT AND MS. LOIS, A SEMI-intimate lunchtime on a Thursday—I wondered if I could call her "Lois," we had something in common, after all, it seemed. Very much executive/secretary from a distance but I could see their lips moving, figures dancing in the viewfinder, zoom lens out as far as it would go, compressing distance. A quick pat here, a shared secret smile there. Who was I to complain about using Margrit? Ms. Harthorne was just more successful with it, I thought glumly.

They waited for the car, Ms. Harthorne with a distinctive case, Gucci logos. They got the BMW, not the limo with the huge thug, and left, Margrit's sloppy driving forcing a delivery truck to brake. After them in the van and what a curious round we made. A fancy jeweler's, that was to be expected, but also a newsstand with porn books in the back section, partitioned off to hide the shame. Quite a journey from Theo's restaurant, where else, I wondered if they'd make the gossip columns, "seen lunching at. . . ," then out the Southwest Freeway at sixty, cursing drivers struggling to get past two mobile roadblocks, the limit ignored here as across the country— why can't laws reflect reality?

It was movie-perfect, the elegant country house well fenced and guarded, and I put a converter on the lens to double its range, looking for a steady rest, the equivalent of five hundred millimeters of telephoto working, distorting the shapes, and I could see the ground heat wavering between me and my quarry. They exited and went inside and I zoomed the street address, giving it more tape time than I needed. They stayed inside for only a few minutes and Ms. Harthorne left *sans* Margrit and drove away, leaving me torn and indecisive. Surely not all this way for an afternooner, it's too complicated for simple pleasures, and I waited, truck backed into obscuring brush, hoping I'd not have to explain the position to a hard-eyed highway patrolman.

Good guess, for Margrit came out with a man, carrying the Gucci briefcase, "Miami Vice" knew what was there, she might as well have made a sign and she got into a brown dusty pickup, nice flash of a leg I knew so well.

Pickups weren't her style and she was awkward with it, over-correcting as she made the turn and I shrank down behind the dash. I had never realized what a lousy driver she was. A quarter mile back on country roads until we arrived at the freeway and then two lanes over and behind, she rarely used her mirror and I felt safe in the tracking van. I was waiting for a stop—a Coke, Margrit, you're thirsty, need some cigs?

I couldn't understand why they were doing this, Houston's decline hurting illegitimate business too? But if they were using her, I was no better because I planned the same. The contents of the briefcase needed examination and I had nothing to fear from her. Beating up on girls is not heroic, though, and my stomach rumbled, wishing for a Rolaid.

She pulled off the freeway at Chimney Rock, zipped across the feeder to a gas station, brand-new, all self-service, tell me again about how you're merely passing increased costs along, dear oil companies, and why self-service is all the rage, no expensive people working to wash your windshield and check your oil. She pulled off to the side and got out with briefcase, this I could see before the lights changed and I had to move off to make the block. And arrived back in time to see her, still with briefcase, climbing back into the truck. Not your style, Margrit, not at all. We went off through suburban streets, amazing number of houses for sale, best investment you can make, right?

I had it all on tape. License numbers, streets, faces as near as possible, but I had consciously hidden Margrit from view, old times' sake, call it what you will. Another briefcase stop, this one a realtor and I was parked in the next driveway, hidden behind black glass, and I got a good close-up of the case, which surely was lighter now as the delivery person made her rounds, what else could she be doing?

I felt uneasy. Margrit was fairly new with them, if very close, and I couldn't see them letting her wander the city with too very much in that case if it was what I thought and that was plastic bags full of cocaine, tightly packed, weighed, and tested, shake the test tube and check the color, high school chemistry nagging at my brain. They wouldn't let her go alone and I would have been obvious to an experienced eye.

So I peeled off and let her go, driving streets in random patterns, watching mirrors, and a blue Ford drifted in my vision, tailing better than I could ever dream of. Watch-dogs.

Two men, faceless behind their dark glasses, always there behind me, why couldn't I watch the mirror better.

"Interesting reversal of roles," I said aloud.

I worked the recorder, replaced the tape I'd shot with another cassette. Then I went to work on the twin latches that held the inside engine cover in place. On a front engine van, the motor protrudes into the passenger compartment and you do service or repairs by removing two hatches on the side of the console, which is usually a piece of fiberglass covered with carpet, housing the radio, a place to put your beer, and so forth. It's simple to get them open when you can crouch down next to the pedals and flip the latches but hell to do while driving. I set the van on cruise headed out Interstate 10, one eye ahead and one down where my hands were working, and I blessed the dark window glass because they couldn't see what I was doing. I got one hatch open finally and wedged the exposed cassette behind the engine, the smell and noise of it filling the truck. It would get hot, there was no helping that, but it would take a good search to find it. I got one latch replaced and said the hell with it, made a U-turn on the feeder, and headed for the Warwick.

The blue Ford followed, closer now, no pretensions.

I had shot maybe two new minutes of tape, when the van's unlocked door was pulled open and one of the guys from the Ford was there. Happily, he was no one I knew and my Beaumont identification was stuffed down in the seat, my newspaper friend's business card, given to me with a sardonic leer that night, in my shirt pocket.

"I like your camera," he said, yanking it away from me.

He liked it so much he busted the catches getting out the cassette, then pulled me from the door and shoved me against the truck, bad breath bouncing from my face.

Shoving, pushing, I was quite tired of this and came off

the truck with a lunge and fiery red splash, blur, pressure, and black. I came to in a minute, both of them in the truck with me, wearing worried looks.

"Why does the newspaper play with video cameras?" one guy asked. Hard hat types, greasy jeans and T-shirts, low-rent muscle, but I never saw the other one come up behind me and I was sick. The other one tossed me my money, held with a paper clip, and I could see enough to realize they hadn't moved the truck. I hoped for newspaper immunity, that's why I'd kept the card, forgive me, old friend, for using you this way. But he was clean and clear, one look at his Irish face and they'd know I'd borrowed the card and his identity.

"I'm doing it on my own," I croaked.

"Doing what," the spokesman asked politely.

"That girl, woman, I knew her from when I was in the PR business, she's a model and I wanted . . ."

"Yes?"

"I wanted, I tried to date her . . ."

"Yes?"

"I wanted some film, tape, of her, I can't help it!"

Did I look enough like a traditional pervert? They were not convinced. The silent one was methodically crushing cassettes, ripping them open with screwdriver and pliers from the glove compartment, trust Vince to be prepared, and pulling out the half-inch tape inside, creasing it between forefinger and thumb—did they think it was film and would be ruined by exposure to light?

"This gets you a little clout, not much," the talkative one said, flipping the business card back to me. "Mostly because it's a pain to get you fired."

"What's her name?" asked the other suddenly.

"Margrit, weird name, but . . . I . . . like her."

They laughed at that, would they buy this stupid story? In the end, I think routine got them, boredom from too many trips in the blue Ford, a few more shoves and threats and they went away, the quiet one making a production of dropping the camera to the pavement as he left.

They felt quite righteous, a whimpy perv in their hands, superiority welcome and they got so involved with explaining how disgusting I was they ignored any threat I could represent. I felt like a particularly loathsome mess they didn't want to clean up and that helped my act. Hell, I was peeping.

I didn't know how I'd explain the camera damage to the rental people but I drove away with only a headache and a lump, male pride somewhat ragged around the edges, you can't have everything, and when I was sure, I retrieved the cassette from the engine compartment and headed for Vince's.

He still wanted to go fishing, his tackle strewn across the office, some people's minds have a single track, but kindly offered to ride with me if I wanted to play detective again. But I had enough tape, that and I didn't want to push my luck. Even the most stubborn weirdo would probably not return and I didn't want to try to explain anything to the blue Ford crew.

I gave him a rain check, explaining that I had to edit.

26

I HAD EDITED ONE OF MY INDUSTRIAL films once, the old way, sixteen-millimeter strips hanging by the dozens from finishing nails, work print, sound-on, shall we cut or dissolve here, lots of arcane grease pencil marks. It wasn't very good.

And in the early days I had fooled around in the studios and control rooms, pathetic technically then, but exciting, a twenty-six-week run of "TV Bingo," boy producer at the board and live commercials.

I had also done a batch of videotape commercials, starting when tape machines were barely existent and if you flubbed the last line you backed up to the front. Then technology overtook me, time base correctors, whirring one-inch tape reels, computerized mixing boards, glowing lights, ultra slo-mo, hard-edge electronic images softened by a diffusion lens.

What I had was raw footage, suspicion, a very active imagination, a doubtful fact or three, and lots of motivation. Still the briefcase was clear and Margrit had been kind enough to show it as she made her rounds, doing Ms. Harthorne's bidding. The boss-lady was clear and sharp and easily recognizable when she handed the case to Margrit, too.

I didn't know the technology but I could draw on a yellow pad and hold it up for the engineers to see, sign language between different cultures, *that's* what you want. I had a due bill, a girl who owed her job to me and she worked the board at a small, private studio, making a living taping bands, would-be MTV all of them, how outrageous can we make this video and catch the fleeting attention of the teen. Out north of town, the Woodlands, giant pines and clean wide streets, massive mixed-use development in the grandest scale, a city built on the edge of the piney woods and well executed at that.

She was glad to see me, even unannounced and with a headache, and we chatted about old times, she was doing well I noted, senior engineer, fat and comfortable with it, jeans stretching across an amazing expanse of bottom.

I happen to know it was metabolism or a curse, she ate mostly salads but never could shrink, her husband seemed happy enough, who was I to pry? And who could care? Lots of worthless people with trim flesh, very few friends of any sex, who could you count on? I thought her lovely.

The problem was the format, half-inch home tape was never designed for editing, and she bounced my footage up to one inch rapidly, stopping at intervals to adjust some knob or that, "Keep the camera steady," she'd say disgustedly. White balance corrected, levels matched, "I've done as much as I can with this, let me call Randy and tell him I'll be late."

We worked until three in the morning and when we were through I had a nice and tight ten-minute show, repetitive probably, no sound-on yet, she didn't need to know what it would say and I had her show me the appropriate buttons and asked her to leave.

"I can't do that."

"You have to, please."

"I don't like any of this, Beaumont. You know I'd do anything for you but I can't leave you in the control room and I need to go home anyhow."

I started out to fake sincere and found I was. My voice cracked a little as I explained enough to make her start to cry, nice woman sees friend smashed and glued together, we've been a mile or two along the track and some of my rage seeped into her. She made some suggestions, rigged a mike for me, wrote out the instructions in case I forgot.

Then she hesitated, not wanting the final jump, "I really shouldn't do this." Half to herself.

"They came into my office and beat me up. They took away my business, kids in school. They tried to drown me in the Gulf and leave me for the crabs, what do you want me to do? Leave?"

And she decided, sweet person that she was, and trundled away from there, indignation apparent from her back, forty pounds less and her body would be as beautiful as her heart.

"Remember to lock up. Mail me the key, remember." I kissed her hard, trying to make gratitude shift from my body to hers, saved my ass once more by knowing good folks.

I do not have an announcer's voice but I had a hell of a script, pecked out on the clumsy non-IBM typewriter the studio's secretary used. Not edited heavily, it came pouring out, facts and suppositions mingled.

I had two tape machines to run, volume to be controlled, and I felt positively space-age, twirling dials. My first audiotape was terrible but then I began to get the hang of levels and where to let the meter needles run and I got something that was ragged enough to be true, matching my jerky video perfectly.

In the end I had a videotape that was not professional but was stronger for all of that, FBI-type footage but with sound and color. I had nothing to show for Bechman, so I ran the first half minute with perfectly black video and his taped voice from that night in the early summer. Then I cut to a shot of Ms. Harthorne entering the BMW with Margrit. That's when my voice-over began and I mixed what I knew for sure with what I thought and supered in the names of companies known to be controlled by American Title Investment Group. I changed my mind and used an old PR photo of Tuckerman from my files to start, "This is a picture of a dead man." Not a bad opening line.

It was a hell of a tape, if I do say so.

The morning sun was coming up and I thought fleetingly of the bay. I'd be at the jetties now, pushing for one last trip if they would have left me alone. I ran the tape one final time, tried to figure out how to make a dub, and gave it up.

I took the single copy, checked out the notes she'd left me so I could shut down the board, managed that, and left, pulling the door to make sure it was locked.

The paperboy on a Honda three-wheeler waved as I wearily went to the truck, another early worker, kid, you seen any worms around these parts?

I figured I was partially home. The tape would cause some stop-and-think and maybe that was enough, surely more weapon than I'd carried up to now, would people believe it?

That's the crucial question, commercial or six-hour special, would they believe it?

It was true but often that's not enough.

27

V<small>INCE AND</small> T<small>AMMY WERE NOT IM</small>-pressed. I got mad, controlling it, the way you do when you sweat to come up with a campaign for a client and he totally misunderstands it. Or, worse, hits you with that magnificent bit of logic: "I don't like it." Control of an advertising budget guarantees good taste and judgment, the ability to visualize, marketing savvy, and an intuitive feel for the marketplace, the knack for sparkling copy.

I had slept away a good part of the day, waking with a dazed, hung-over feeling, disoriented, and out of synch. I called the meeting for as soon as Tammy could get there after work and we screened the video at Vince's place, before official opening.

"It's . . . interesting," she said politely.

"They'll blow you out of the water," Vince said.

I bit back what I wanted to say, which was at least partially a wail, and considered their comments. It's always tough when you put people in the judge's role, because it distorts their response. "Show this to the secretaries!" is enough to drive an adperson to drink. "I'll take it home and show the wife" is worse.

"Okay," I said, "it's not '60 Minutes.' But think of this. Remember when the video bandit guy interrupted the cable broadcast? It made *Time* magazine and the wire services. All he broadcast was a written message."

"So?" they asked, in unison.

"So if Ms. Harthorne thinks I can get this on the tube, in X thousands of households, maybe she'll want to come to the table."

"Or maybe she'll get a thug to rap you on the head," Vince said dryly.

A damn-near-naked girl came in and complained to Vince about her check. Seems that she had two exemptions and wasn't getting them and would he *please* help her.

Tammy peered around her to ask why I was insisting on *fighting* with these people. Vince gave the girl some money and told her he'd straighten everything out.

"I don't want to," I said. "I'm a devout coward, actually, but I don't see that I have a choice. They're going to fix me good. Besides, they've already had enough good swings at me, they're not getting any more for free."

"Run it again," said Vince.

We looked at the tape again and I was terribly conscious of the sheer amateurishness of it, things any first-year film student could have done better, and I was oddly defensive. The silence was hard to take.

"It's not that awful," I said.

"No, I'm thinking of it at home, on TV," Tammy said. "The *idea* that somebody pirated time to play this is probably more important than what it says," I said. "Medium and message, see?"

"I thought the cable companies had super-duper scramblers, or something," Vince said.

"Hell, I don't know," I said, discouraged. "Anybody got a better idea?"

"If they can scramble, actually I think it's a code, then somebody else can unscramble," Tammy said loyally.

"I don't think scramblers or no scramblers is the problem here. If I have to try to air it, the blackmail isn't working. Besides, they scramble the signals going out of the studio, I can make a try to get in ahead of that," I said wearily.

Another dancer appeared at Vince's door in a terry-cloth robe she had forgotten to belt. I was not cheered but looked anyway and Tammy kicked me sharply. "Pay attention."

"I *am* paying attention," I said.

Vince walked out to settle whatever problem was brewing and I looked at Tammy and shrugged. "What can I say? I've got to do something."

"Think it through. You show this or threaten to show it?"

"Threaten, at first, I suppose."

"And then what?"

"And then, she either agrees to let me alone or she calls my bluff. At that point the ball is really in my court."

"How do you do this? A note cut from the newspaper?"

"No, a meeting, I think. Preview showing."

"How about we just catch this broad in the car and talk some serious sense to her," said Vince from the door.

"I can't do that, I don't know how," I said, feeling less than a man.

Tammy patted me on the arm. Vince shrugged and disappeared. I fixed a drink. We sat for a minute and Tammy asked me, "Is that all you want, to be left alone?"

"It seems rather a lot."

"What about our business? What about the office? What about the pain and suffering? What about all that!"

"Let's not push our luck."

"You know," she said, "sometimes you're a real pussy."

On that happy note, we broke up the meeting. I took the tape from Vince's machine and we went down the hall to find him to say good-night. I noticed Tammy eyeing the dancers speculatively and I suppose she was comparing. I thought she looked wonderful. Told her so.

As we walked out to the cars, I told her again. It was true, what the hell. She angled for a thank-you kiss and I obliged, forgetting my resolve. Then I kissed her back, surprised when she didn't flinch or draw away. Somehow we were in the car, bumped my head, no problem though it hurt.

We started necking there in the parking lot, her idea, return with us now to those wondrous days of yesteryear. I found myself working on kissing right, hands touching, nothing below the waist, steamy breath, panting a bit, damn steering column in the way.

"Jesus," I said. "Wait a minute. This won't play."

"Why not?"

"Because it won't that's all!" I was upset. "It's a dumb idea, I'm sorry, I was stupid. Jesus! You'd think I'd grow up, I'm sorry."

"I'm not," she said, and slid out the door to get to her own car. "Are you coming over to my house?"

"No, hell no! You think I'm nuts?" I would have got out to make the points more emphatically, but she was too close and I didn't really want to do any more kissing because I was on the ragged edge already. Stupid thing.

"I think you're nuts if you don't," she said softly, lots of straight-on eye contact, what was I supposed to do? "Tammy . . ." I wailed.

She shrugged and went to her car and drove away, no

hesitation. Kid was straightforward enough. Maybe I should follow her home, protect her. I laughed sourly at myself. Then I went back inside and sat down and waited for Saki, trying to adjust my brain. I slipped and called her "Tammy," which made her order drinks at a furious rate, my tab.

In the morning, I got myself sorted out and called Margrit from the motel. I couldn't get through and I left my name but told them I was calling from a pay phone and would call back. On the return call, I got her and she was curiously subdued.

"I can't see you," she said.

"Demands of the job, right?"

"I'm very busy, we all are, what can I do for you?"

"I need to see Lois. Excuse me, Ms. Harthorne."

"Why? She won't see you. We're very busy."

"Margrit," I said. "You've known me a long time and we've been through a lot. I've got one or two coming, wouldn't you say?"

"That has nothing to do with now," she said dully.

"I need to see Ms. Harthorne and I promise you she wants to hear what I've got to say."

"I can tell her. What time can you be here?"

"I'm not coming there, it will have to be outside."

"Beaumont," she said. "This is the Warwick. What could happen to you at the Warwick?"

"I don't plan on finding out."

"Then I can't . . ."

I interrupted. "Tell her this. Tell her there's a whole lot of unfavorable publicity, some film she doesn't know about, videotape actually, and if she wants to avoid publicity, she needs to talk to me."

Ms. Harthorne came on the line unexpectedly. Her voice was as calm as ever, without expression. "Surely you're not considering negative advertising, Mr. Beaumont?"

"Hello again," I said with the best imitation of good cheer I could muster. "No, I'm not. But there are some things better not held up for public examination, wouldn't you agree?"

"Perhaps."

"In any event, what can happen? Bring the monster."

"Robert would not be amused, Mr. Beaumont."

"Look," I said. "You guys have been nothing but grief for me. All I want is a clean bill of health. You can do it with a phone call. I just want to give you a reason to make the phone call, all right?"

"I believe that's called blackmail, Mr. Beaumont, and the authorities frown on it."

"Blackmail is when you ask for something. What I'm asking is not something."

"Suppose I assured you . . ."

"Don't bother," I interrupted. "Would you like to see what I've got?" I could feel her shudder. "The materials I mentioned."

"You will be contacted at the motel, Room 305 I believe."

And she hung up and left me staring at a dead phone. I got out of the motel like a shot, bags stuffed, they could keep the extra few days rent. That woman scared the excrement out of me and I damn near broke my neck looking for tails. I finally ended up way out west of town, off I-10, where they had put the streets in for a new subdivision on the empty prairie and I looked around and around but I was all alone.

Don't poke at the tigers unless you're sure of the cage. But they wouldn't leave me alone. My videotape and careful planning seemed childish and I couldn't see anyone around but I was cold with fear.

"Why me?" I said to the sky. Nobody answered.

28

I COULDN'T STAY OUT OF THE BALD prairie. There's a ton of that west of Houston and I could see for miles. I admired the skill of the contractors, who had done their job and left very fine streets with curbs and gutters all clean and new, cutting through nowhere to no place. Seemed safe and peaceful. Yet I remembered the guys in the blue Ford who would not be so easy on me this time and I didn't want to move. I could see tiny cars moving on I-10 and I'd catch the roaring of a big semi now and then when the wind was blowing right and I didn't want to move. "I would be contacted" or not: I wanted to keep the ball in my court.

There was another car off in the distance, heading generally in my direction, over in another section of the acreage that some poor developer had planned to make his fortune. Probably a bargain hunter, deep of pocket, wanting to get the land for its raw-dirt value, never mind those handsome streets and the permits and the easements, property rights, endless legal squabbles to get a project off the ground. We were critical of developers on aesthetic grounds and too often we were right, but I still marveled at the stubborn fight it took to get through all the paper and get something built. No small achievement that. Only money supplies that kind of motivation. Perhaps love.

Two men got out and paced off something in the distance, probably an anxious owner trying to conceal his need and a hard-eyed buyer looking for a deal. Houston's depression would be the start of a whole new batch of family fortunes, a new money-elite to replace the oil wealth. Buy at the bottom, sell at the top. Easier to do when you have money. They disappeared behind their car and from my mind and I tried to think of the best thing to do. Absently I noted that the second engine compartment latch had never been secured and bent to do that. I could stay out here in the boonies . . .

The windshield shattered with a horrible bang, instant craze of cracks radiating outward from a saucepan-sized hole right where my head had been and I started the van still below the dash, seven hundred pounds of cast-iron engine block between me and the rifleman, and I risked a peek, thankful for the broad empty streets, and pushed the accelerator through the floorboards. The side window behind me went with a crash, different tone coming from the broad expanse of darkened glass, and I was well over fifty on what would have been suburban streets, tough target and I didn't know where I was going but jumped a curb and tore across an empty intersection trying to hold the van on the road and get the glass out of my hair and his third and fourth shots must have missed entirely, wild van a bad target, deflection, angle, increasing distance. Stop me for reckless driving, please.

I had to make a conscious effort to control my bladder, bouncing truck making it worse. The brute violence of glass bursting inward, like somebody had taken a full swing with a ten-pound sledge, made me shake inside. Somewhere I was amazed and a bit proud of my reflexes, no combat training but not a bad reaction. I wanted to scream, "Wait!" dissuade them from this madness, not precious me!

I emerged somewhere near Simonton, tiny bedroom town of the wealthy, and I stopped beneath the shade of a pro-Houston billboard and shook a bit. I saw no signs of the rifleman/land buyer I had let get too close and anything that moved would make me start. The pro-Houston stuff was the city's attempt at false good cheer, that's a cynical view surely, yet the boosterism had a hollow flavor to it. It was everywhere, donated billboard space and radio spots, a TV special soon.

I went back to the city—where else was I to go?

Vince would not be pleased with the condition of his van and I knocked out the broken windows underneath the billboard's shade. It would be breezy but call less attention and for the first time in my life I wished I were small and indistinguishable, an accountant or something, narrow tie, cheap shirts, one of thousands coming out of a downtown building at 5:02, just let me melt into the crowds, please, no questions asked. I was violently sick beside the road. The goddamn confident gall of them, the balls. A sunny Texas day, let's go Beaumont hunting, just outside the city limits. My threats to Ms. Harthorne bounced in my memory, no wonder she ignored me. Live bait doesn't get to protest when the steel hook curves through the spine.

If life is an endless series of near-infinite choices and each of them changes the course of it, I wished that paper back in Tuckerman's folder more than I had wished for anything, bar nothing, lust or Christmas presents, shiny new bike or lovely unobtainable girl, dying in a state of grace, full head of hair. I was ruined by a bit of sticky tape, there to protect a piece of art now useless, ad's run, who cares?

I got to Vince's place with the last of the daylight and went to the back and for the first time he did not unlock the door to see who was there but called through it in a strange voice. I told him it was me and the door opened grudgingly and Vince was standing there, heavy metal in his fist, barrel steady as a rock. I was sick of guns, especially aimed at me. I didn't move until he nodded.

My old friend had suffered.

The fist that held the gun was torn and bloody still, paper towels wrapped around it seeping red, and his face was mashed. He held himself stiffly and I could only guess at the pain he was in, shirt sleeve torn, *both* hands torn up, all his teeth visible when he smiled but redness oozing through the cracks.

"I should see the other guy?" I asked.

"I hope I see him first." And there was no mistaking his meaning, a score to be settled, why did he put up with me, deep weariness creeping through my bones, too much to ask to be a friend of me, goddamn them all.

"Robert?"

"If Robert is a great big dead man walking 'round," he said, leading me to the office, and I wanted to fuss over him, fix the wounds, some pathetic expression of my shame, and he shrugged me off and poured drinks.

"I've had worse than this on a good Saturday night," he said.

But the cold liquid hurt and burned his mouth and he moved stiffly, not the smooth flowing motions of the Vince I knew, and I suggested a hospital, imagining broken ribs grating, jagged edges tearing inside the skin's shell. He was having none of that, not false pride but a cold assessment of the damages, a wealth of experience doing the diagnosis.

"Nothing's broke. Said he was a friend of yours. Looked like an NFL lineman," he said. "Know him?"

"I know him but he's lying." It wasn't Robert, then.

"Yeah."

"They want me bad, damnit why? I'm no threat anymore, never was, why all this shit?"

"I hurt him," Vince said. "Hurt him bad. God, it was like hitting a brick wall, no neck to speak of when I got an arm around him."

My head came up and I described my caller from a century ago, when I was still in business, the Xerox breaker that Mr. Evans had held at shotgun point with Court. It sounded like the same guy and then I described Robert and we got thoroughly mixed up.

"Doesn't matter," said Vince. "I see him and he's dead and we can sort out who he is later."

"Jesus, Vince," I said, "if they know you, they know Tammy too!" And I dived for the phone and waited out the anxious rings until she came on shaky-voiced, and I told her it was me and she started to cry. Seven kinds of a shit, old Beaumont brings joy to all his friends. No-Neck had been there too, no Court to accompany and restrain him but he hadn't hurt her, unless you count the psychic scars. Young pretty girl, a smile forgives you a bump of the car ahead, a look gets you through, everybody worships you in his own way, sheer niceness coming through. Happy, sunlight girl until a No-Neck forces his way in and makes some ugly threats, uglier because they're true and *possible*. He makes you feel they're possible and robs away a very valuable thing, a confidence unshakable till now, another gift for knowing me. A simple shove could do it, my God, he could break her in half, physical superiority wins again and you can take your logic and moral advantages and with six bits buy coffee.

"I want to stay with you tonight, but I'm afraid to leave," she said with tears. "I'm afraid."

"We'll get you something better," I said. "I'll be there in fifteen minutes." Vince was already moving toward the door. He asked me to drive and noted the windows of the van sourly and we took his car, four doors, no distinguishing marks, power everything.

Vince's plastic got her space at a downtown hotel, twenty stories of anonymous rooms, she could call in sick in the morning, use room service, and keep the chain on the door. She didn't want to stay and she wanted to nurse the wounds and she was mad and scared, all mixed up into confusion, and I got the phone and ordered a bottle of vodka and mixers and told her to drink until she could sleep and *not to leave the room.*

"Now head to the Y," he said when we got the car back from the garage. Downtown YMCA, greasy old building, endless series of renovations, a rabbit warren of racquetball courts and a sullen smell hanging in the halls. Everybody was fit and trim, T-shirts molded to firm bodies, and I felt clumsy, sitting beside the whirlpool tub looking at the black marks on Vince's ribs. He claimed it made him feel like new and he did move better but I doubted that he'd want to run a pass route right this minute and said so.

"Now, Beaumont," he said, "we get to some serious drinking." And he had me drive him home, a privilege never before granted in nearly twenty years of knowing him. West University, sleepy fifties homes near Rice University, very chichi and very nice, give the trees some time to grow and they'll turn any neighborhood into some place where you'd want to stay. Nice houses too, a mix, and Vince's was two stories fronting on a quiet street with esplanades, neighbors the powers that be who stayed out of newspapers and overall a quiet air of luxury.

"Bought it when it was cheap," he said, showing me

hardwood floors and ten-foot ceilings, a magnificent old glass chandelier, arched doorways, and the rest.

We sat with the bottles on the table and the TV flickering in the wall, twenty-five-inch set and all the gadgets mounted in stained hardwood and complete with sliding doors to put the whole thing out of mind.

"I think we need a final solution," he said three drinks later. "Some way to cut all this shit and get back to normal. I'm getting too old to enjoy this."

"I don't feel right for offering an opinion," I said quietly. "My ribs don't hurt, you're taking the injuries."

"Good Christ, Beaumont!" he exploded, and winced. "What about your business, what about Margrit? What about the holes that would be in you right now if you hadn't ducked. Jesus!"

I started to say something and he told me to can the false modesty and concentrate on getting out.

"They're in business, just like me," I said slowly. "That's the truth. I need to show them that it's unprofitable to do business like they're doing, that's all. God, they must have something better to do. I just need to show them that chasing me isn't smart, that's all."

"That seems to be plenty," Vince said.

"There's no reason for all of this," I said. "The original point was that I did some snooping—did I tell you about the snooping?—and found out something I shouldn't but that's dead and gone now. Surely."

"The snowball's rolling downhill."

"No," I said. "That doesn't make sense. No matter how big they are, by now somebody would tell them it's counter-productive."

"The insurance company's not going to believe me about the van," Vince said.

"I was always polite to Ms. Harthorne, too," I said. "Margrit says she's horribly busy, why are they fucking with me?"

"Practice, maybe," said Vince. "I'm going to bed."

29

I WAS PRO-HOUSTON, YES I WAS,
risking a public appearance or semipublic appearance to
do it, finding an old acquaintance frantic with last-minute
worries about his TV special and taking some of the burden off his hands by writing press releases and scheduling
some photography. I was a helpful Beaumont, boosting
the city with the best of them, and what I wanted was
access to the control room. I never voiced my private
thoughts which revolved around the boosterism futility of
showing a pro-Houston special in Houston.

But I could get into the control room, the place where
they send out the mysterious signals which make us laugh
along with the sound track mirth during prime time each
evening.

Not an easy thing to get at, that, everybody loves TV,

excitement showbiz, crazy people with funny hair and a whole new lingo. Cross-dissolving, riding gains, and targeting audiences with the best of them I got in there with the frenetic party putting the last-minute touches on the tape, even watched the preview showing from the safety of the booth, Ms. Harthorne among the dignitaries in the studio audience, splendid raw silk dress, where was Margrit?

Twenty years in the business proving its worth after all, perhaps they thought me an old has-been sniffing around for a dropped tidbit but they let me in when I demonstrated I'd work for free and didn't mind the scut, if scut was what needed doing. I knew some of them of course, engineers who I had helped break in the first tape machines, an audio guy with a most peculiar manner of speech. Plus new ones, of course, who mostly ignored me but let me sit in the background. TV people by and large being among the nicest in the business, they let me in and I picked up a clipboard and pretended to be important or at least part of the deal.

In a day's time nobody bothered me but I kept the clipboard.

Vince had let me stay in a great old guest bedroom, off to the side on the second story, genuine four-poster and comforter and I suspect nobody slept as well. Tammy was sick of the hotel but we wouldn't let her leave and when I mentioned the tab to Vince and my inability to pay him back he gave me a black look and I shut up. He kept different hours because of the club and was moving easily now, his face still a mess but nobody kidded him about it, especially me.

The third day was the showing and I made myself invisible as much as possible, clutching my notes and trying to get a handle on the actual broadcast. The dignitaries were gone, of course, preview-showing people, got to stay ahead of the masses. I could visualize them dropping a hint or two, "Nice piece of work, actually," to their friends gathered around the big-screen projection television set to see Houston Proud.

It *was* a nice tape, demonstrating the good things about the city, citing statistics, showing potentials, proving beyond a doubt that we were still a market to be reckoned with. I still privately felt it would have been better shown elsewhere, in the affluent-again Eastern states, for example, but I kept my counsel and tried to look busy. Hell, I would have run ads citing the class A office space available and its price and that alone probably would have caused a rash of industrial relocations, jobs, prosperity, Michigan plates on the freeway. I thought it best not to mention this concept.

The mechanics were in my favor. The tape would be originated from the very control room in which I sat, clipboard near but careful not to touch any of the banks of switches or glowing little lights, and beamed to the three VHF stations live. Cable companies would get a signal bounced to their satellites and bounced down to their audiences. Two people, perhaps only one at times, would be there and the station manager in the viewing room down the hall. Perhaps a stray dignitary or two. But there were only two people in the control room and it had a heavy, soundproof door. I sat with them looking important and making notes on the final run-through, an hour before broadcast time and it was a good tape, we all agreed to that. At the end, the engineer/director froze the line monitor and the other eight sets were dead, although one still showed a local logo, left over from taping a commercial, and I wanted to be back in the agency business.

"I'll see you when we go on the air," I said to the engineer, one of the new breed who had seen me chatting with his boss and wandering the halls for the past two days. He waved an acknowledgment and adjusted something. One hour.

I found a phone and called Vince.

He didn't understand the plan but agreed to come and I waited outside for him, checking my watch every five minutes. When he pulled up I steered him to the employee's coffee bar and we drank a Tab, pretending to be busy when somebody came in.

"Big night, eh?" said a guy I knew vaguely, a time salesman who used to call on me. He wanted to chat and I introduced Vince as an account executive with GS&W and the salesman looked puzzled but wouldn't leave. You could see him racking his brains for GS&W, Goodrich, Spenser & Who? He wouldn't leave and at five minutes to airtime, I suggested to Vince we had to go and shook the salesman's hand vigorously.

"Enjoy it," I said. "It's going to be quite a show."

We took our positions in the control room and I straightened up the viewing area, ignored by the director who was having an incomprehensible discussion with the sound man over headphones, so we only heard half of the conversation. I put a fresh, clean ashtray by his hand and he nodded thanks.

We counted down, "Just like on TV," whispered Vince, and the show was on the air. Three minutes in, the director and his sound man were both secure, bound, and on the floor, and I frantically was trying to make some sense out of the mixing board.

My tape was cued and ready, a bonus I'd received when the engineer left the room to pee, and I slipped the cassette into an unused machine, but I couldn't find the switch to get it on the air. Vince stood by the door and radiated impatience. Houston Proud rolled on.

My tape was frozen, first frame on the preview monitors. The engineer and sound man had not made any fuss, a threat or two, but Vince's battered face was a great convincer and he held his hand in his pocket nicely. I didn't ask if the gun was there, I didn't want to know.

The mixing board was like a space shuttle, dials and switches, a joystick, rows and rows of lights and buttons. All I had to do was discover how to feed my tape to the live broadcast in place of what was scheduled. But I was afraid to move things indiscriminately, screwing up the show before my tape ran because that would lead to a herd of tech people in the control room before I could get my stuff on the air.

"Hurry," Vince said.

"I'm trying. I can't figure this fucker out!"

He bent and dragged up the engineer and pulled him over to the board. I was impressed because Vince handled a full-size man like a toddler. I was still not up to speed on physical violence and its efficiency.

"Show him!" he said.

"Hit the preview button," said the engineer, Frank I think it was, after a quick look into Vince's eyes.

"Show me," I said, and he did and the images flickered on the screens. I turned and looked, then turned back to the engineer. Teach you to wear a tie, sorry it's all crumpled around your wrists. "Now what?"

"Push that lever upward and you're on the air." I took a breath and did it and the line monitor showed my videotape, volume blasting through the speakers. The needles jumped into the red and slammed against the pegs.

"Turn it down," yelled Vince.

"That red knob," said the engineer, and I made the adjustment and stopped to watch my handiwork. They'd write about this tomorrow and I'd never get into another studio in Houston and it was a shame, but anybody has a limit and I was well past mine. So long, career, so long, ad biz.

I wanted to stay and watch, fascinated by a lifelong dream happening, even if the circumstances were less than ideal. I had hoped for a Hollywood opening but what the hell.

Vince was having none of this and pulled me from the control room. We left both technicians out of sight and locked the heavy door, breaking the key off in it.

"About three minutes to get through," Vince said.

"Hell, the whole show is less than ten," I said as we were running down the hall. I could hear the shouts coming from the executive viewing room already. I wondered what the scene was at the VHF stations, would the engineers be caught napping or would they switch immediately to Network Transmission Temporarily Interrupted cards?

"It's not network, so what card will they use?" I asked Vince as we were getting into the car. He looked at me, started up, and drove away.

"Stop the car, I've got to make a call," I said like an idiot, and he shook his head and drove directly to the Foxy Lady.

Once inside his office, I dialed for Ms. Harthorne and told the guy my name. She came on the line quickly.

"You are an utter imbecile," she said. "Our organization has had no interest in you for months! None."

"So who's shooting out the windows of . . ."

"Your miserable life is of no concern to me," she said. "Nor your friends, who'll suffer for knowing you. You haven't heard the last of us. You fool!"

As usual, she hung up in the middle of my next sentence and I turned to Vince and said, "She says it's not her."

"That's what they all say," he replied.

I was mostly convinced and this opened up a whole new area of worry. Not a single person in the club had seen the show so I couldn't get a critique, either.

About an hour later, a cab driver came into the Foxy Lady and was directed to my table. He came up, black face among a fair to middlin' crowd of whites, and told me there was a lady waiting outside for me.

I didn't want to go but I did.

I~T~ ~WAS~ ~WORSE~ ~BECAUSE~ ~IT~ ~WAS~
Margrit. She wasn't hurt all that bad, Vince's injuries
would have put her in the hospital for a month, but the
idea of being hurt, that it was possible and casually ac-
complished, had reduced her to a pathetic shadow of herself. Her pretty bluster was the worse. I thought of
Tammy, safe I hoped, and took Margrit inside with me.

The cabbie wanted a little less than seven and I gave
him ten, overtipping again, and took her to the office. She
was scratched and a black eye would show up in the
morning, she had a bruise on her ribs and had to show us
that, no bra, good breasts. But we were in a veritable field
of good breasts and it was less than exciting and she
sensed that and rearranged her clothes.

She couldn't find a comfortable role to play. I was the

rotten monster of all time at first and then she was actually working for me, boring from within, trying to help on the inside. She was joyful, she sobbed unexpectedly, and overall she bore her crisis poorly.

After every comment, she'd glance a quick sidelong glance, trying to get a reaction, some cue to show her how she should play this. And when the attention shifted away from her, she'd start to remember, and I could see her shake, Tammy all over again, yet Margrit had less to fall back upon, convictions of her worth less solidly rooted.

I felt responsible, of course.

The phone rang among all this, Vince answered and gave it to me. It was Tammy, from the hotel, and she was bubbling.

"In-fucking-credible!" she said.

"You saw the show, then?"

"Un-bloody-believable! I was sitting around, you remember I'm marooned at the Hyatt and need out, hint hint, anyhow I was sitting there watching the tube, thinking about calling Room Service *again* and here comes the skyline shot and all this stuff about Houston and then . . ."

"I forgot to put titles on the tape."

"Yeah. But blamn! Here comes this black-and-white photo of Mr. Tuckerman . . ."

"The late Mr. Tuckerman . . ."

"Right, right. And it was you. I recognized your voice. And all this stuff comes on about American Group, American Title, whatever, and they put up the slide they use, you know? And then they start showing your stuff again but only for about thirty seconds and it goes blank!"

"Damn," I said. "I guess that means people really didn't get the message."

"No, no! They got to the part about American Title being under investigation and the stuff about Tuckerman, and some of the stuff about you. They ran two minutes or more."

I was oddly deflated. I had packed the tape inverted-pyramid-style, putting as much of the information as I could up front, but there was enough to fill up the full ten minutes. I guess it was too much to hope that the whole tape played. And that was my only copy. Tammy told me the thing had made the ten o'clock news and the announcers couldn't decide whether to treat it as a prank or be serious. The FCC would investigate. The DA had no comment. The engineer just waved and grinned, unused to being on that side of the camera. The station manager gave me a hard time. Nobody from America Title Investment Group was available. References to the HBO bandit were common.

"Did they get the idea that these guys were illegal, violent, and dangerous?" I asked Tammy.

"I did," she said.

"Yeah, but you know."

"Our favorite lady said she had nothing to do with all the shit I've been having but she was going to get me," I said gloomily. "I wonder what she thinks she's *been* doing."

I could hear a commotion out front and one of the dancers came running into Vince's office yelling something about the "TV being here!" and I said, "Oh, shit," and hung up.

They were there, all right, typical scraggly cameraman and the plastic announcer, female in this case, and the lights were blinding and I tried not to squint. I did three "No comments" and two "I don't knows" and looked predictably stupid. Here was my big chance and I was acting like a civilian. I'd been on camera a dozen times before and I felt guilty. I looked guilty.

Hell, I was guilty.

The interview was not going well and the announcer person was about to wrap it up, disgust dribbling from the corner of her mouth, when I had an inspiration.

"Yes, I made that tape," I said. "And sneaked it on the

air. I did it because I had to and I'm sorry it was neces-
sary. The people in the tape are not . . . good for the city.
Certainly not good for me. They have a vendetta going.''
The cameraman, grinning, zoomed me for a pore shot.
''The tape tells you something, something ugly, something
the authorities have been trying to prove, legally, for some
time. I don't have to prove anything according to the . . .
Rules of Evidence. I can just make a videotape.''

The newslady said something but I couldn't make it
out. I plunged ahead.

''I believe,'' I said to the camera, projecting simple honesty, ''that the only sensible thing would be to air the
whole tape and see if the allegations have any basis in
fact. That's a sure defense against slander. Or is it libel, I
can never remember.''

She broke up and some enterprising fellow had T-shirts
out within three days: ''Libel or Slander? I Can't Remember.''

I hope he made a fortune.

The photos that made the papers the next morning (I
broke my rule about reading the evening paper in the A.M.)
had me and two of Vince's more presentable dancers and
out-of-context quotes. I was ''an independent businessman,'' ''an unemployed writer,'' and a ''small ad
agency owner.''

I was six-two and a fraction and the agency was long
gone but that didn't bother the newspaper. I decided to
put Margrit under my arm and head for the bay.

Somebody would screen the tape, my old reporter
friend turned-executive or his minions was my bet, because I had shown him up a bit, desperation strikes again.

Maybe I could keep my clippings and show them to the
next assassin they sent. Or perhaps they wouldn't send an
assassin at all, it's a deed best done away from the light of
day.

Nobody did anything official, at least for now. The station's security people wanted to make it all go away, the grand jury was tied up with a particularly juicy murder and Ms. Harthorne probably still believed in cutting out the legal middlemen. Nobody arrested me, in any event. And I stayed at Vince's so the papers couldn't reach me for further quotes. Fame is fleeting, sure enough.

They should have left me alone, that's all it would have taken, but I took a perverse pride in Beaumont's Famous Pirate Job even if only a couple of minutes hit the air. Mess with me and I'll hit you with an adjective or dump a whole lot of press releases on your head.

I had to do something with Margrit. Nobody else had volunteered. Ever made a mistake, realized you were doing it, and gone ahead anyhow? I felt responsible for her joblessness, even though she may have owed the position, perversely, to Ms. Harthorne's rage at me. Maybe we both could change, such lies we tell ourselves. "You obviously need someplace to go," I said to her, and she nodded, a single suitcase outside the door.

We didn't talk much on the way to the bay. She did say, out of nowhere, that she planned on using the ATIG American Express card a lot and I reminded her of No-Neck, which probably killed that idea.

31

It wasn't a big enough story to keep sending down reporters to Point Lookout. Most of the Houston Proud bunch wanted to lynch me but they were essentially nonviolent types. The engineer whom we had tied up got a promotion but I don't know what happened to the sound man, sound guys are usually a bit obscure anyway.

Time had some admonishing thoughts and *Newsweek* gave it a paragraph, the business press talked about the sanctity of the commercial airwaves which means they never had any dealings with a time salesman. Overall, I was both hero and goat and frequently both in the same news story. The good news was, as far as I was concerned, that my tape had stirred up a reasonable amount of heat on Ms. Harthorne and the American Title bunch. Another grand jury, the state attorney general (a publicity hound), some obscure branch of the Feds, everybody would look into it. I fantasized about public humiliation for Ms. Harthorne, but decided that my brief career in the spotlight would best be over. Quit While Ahead is a reasonable motto. But the attendant publicity, the ongoing investigations, and the editorials probably would keep me out of trouble for a while.

It would be bad for their business.

Tammy had cabbed over to Vince's club on the night of the broadcast, full of enthusiasm and hugs and kisses and babblings. Unfortunately she was wrapped around my neck when Margrit emerged from the Ladies' and there was a brief but unpleasant scene.

When I tried to explain that I was taking Margrit to the bay for therapy, Tammy had been polite. Period. She disappeared in the melee and was busy when I tried to call her later. Once more I found myself doing something I didn't really want to, Hector Edfelter's words of wisdom to the contrary, and it was costing me. I kept thinking about Ms. Harthorne's claim of no interest, even though Vince shrugged it off. *Somebody* had taken a shot at me on the prairie east of Katy. And here I was, broke, with the wrong girl at the bay.

Margrit was bitchy. As always when she was bitchy, she was never in the mood and managed to pour herself into bed early every night. I had interrupted her career. I was always going to be small time. I had fucked up.

Frequently, I agreed with her.

I called Tammy from Evans's house and listened to the phone buzz. I tried a dozen times and she was never there. I should have called in the middle of the night but was too drunk. It was a helluva fall for the bay fish, warm and still, and I spent days in salt water up to my waist. Margrit borrowed the car to go to Port Lavaca a lot.

And Ms. Harthorne said it wasn't them.

I followed what story there was to follow in the *Victoria Advocate* and was pleased to see their troubles were multiplying. The rat pack syndrome, everybody wanted a piece of the action and nice black newspaper ink. Newspaper photos grew unpleasant captions, investigations were proceeding, indictments were coming down like hail. Prominent people were scurrying like mad to disassociate themselves, Ms. Harthorne emerging from the federal courthouse, TV reporters looking serious.

It didn't help any when they dug up Tuckerman's death and reinvestigated it, although Margrit swore, when she would talk to me, that they told her it was an accident. It further didn't help when their porn newsstand guy shot and wounded an off-duty cop perusing the flesh material in the back, under the premise that he was there for the receipts, not the bare bodies.

I got lost in the shuffle, a few ominous phone calls, "Need you to testify," regulation X of the Federal Communications Commission of the U.S., probably take my VHF license away if I weren't careful. But I had started this particular snowball on its downhill ride and the enthusiasm to prosecute was lacking. I did get notice of a hearing. And at times I gloated a little, to myself only, usually at night, when only God could witness my immodesty. A small gloat only and a knock-on-wood.

Things were too bad to last. Margrit was gone, God knows where, the night I got the call, Evans emerging from the black night when I was upstairs on the deck with bourbon.

"Call for you," he said unseen.

"Thanks," I said. "Is it Houston?"

"Yep."

I hurried across the hundred yards between our houses, skirting their little garden and walking wide around snake-filled piles of wood, Bullit frolicking around my feet. She had made friends with the cats, the can't-beat-'em philosophy, and one crawled out from beneath the house to greet us. Stupid dog.

It wasn't Tammy.

Instead it was a brand-new male voice, carefully legal, rehearsed words, somewhat subdued, formal phrasing, a loathing crawling beneath there someplace, he understood that they had "inadvertently" caused some business harm, perhaps coincidental. Was I planning any action?

Action as in lawsuit?

"It's something that we are aware of, although we would vigorously defend against it, no real cause, courts would find it without merit in the opinion of our counsel."

"You're afraid I'm going to sue." The idea was brand-new to me, old-fashioned I guess, suing had never crossed my mind. Not a way I care to handle problems, twenty years in business and never found it necessary, take your chances and your lumps and cry about it quietly. But I could play the game.

I said, after the proper nervous-making pause, "The possibility has, of course, crossed my mind. My dealings with Ms. Harthorne and American Title were . . . unfortunate . . . I was done actual, provable damage, we both know that."

"Not at all," he said stiffly.

"Well, the damage happened, I, ah . . . my business went from fair to awful rather fast, I'm sure there's a trace or two of evidence why it happened, wouldn't you guess?" I was fishing now, the bait launched gently against the cutbank grass, cork twitching, would he bite?

"I would be grateful if you'd sign a waiver."

"And what would I be waiving?" I asked, hoping for an admission.

"Any rights you have to bring action against us, a 'hold harmless' document, as we attorneys say."

We waited for a silent moment, Evans and "the wife" watching the big TV, a dish receiver locked in on a satellite a thousand miles up, Point Lookout and man in space, an unlikely marriage. He called her that, in the third person, but he also knew who had made their deal work, all the years and crazy airplanes, combat pay and all. He loved her. I was trying to feel my way on a shifty bottom with my caller.

"Why would I sign this document, not being an attorney?"

"Because you've been mistaken," he said sharply. "Wrong, wrong all along."

"In that case, what are you worried about?"

"Mr. Beaumont, I'm sure you're aware of the concept of a nuisance suit. You are also aware of the considerable publicity, most of it totally meaningless and out of proportion, we have been receiving."

"I don't get the Houston papers anymore," I lied. "Have you been getting a lot of press coverage?"

"That is of no matter here. We operate most efficiently when we are able to conduct our entirely legitimate business outside of the glare of publicity. Not to mention the legal expense and the enormous loss of time."

"I understand that," I said. "I used to have a business. But what about the illegitimate part?"

He didn't answer that and waited. I was scaring the fish.

"What specifically are you proposing?"

He was glad to get to it, this phone call churning bile in his elegant stomach I suspected, "We would like you to sign the waiver and agree to absolutely no publicity in any matter related to us. No interviews, publicity of any sort."

"About your company only," I said slowly.

"And about your illegal activities at the studio, any matters in conjunction with that too."

"I can't control what they write."

"You can control what they have to write about."

"Okay," I said. "I do this and sign your waiver and what do I get?" Evans looked up from the TV and smiled a sleepy smile.

"We are advised a lump-sum payment could be made, the payment to be covered by the same waiver, that is, also not to be mentioned."

"Except to the IRS."

"That's entirely your affair. The waiver would carry certain penalties under law, of course."

"How much?" I asked baldly.

He named a number and it was twice what I would net in a year and I was tempted to push for more, sell out if you must but get a good price. Instead, I told him I would have to talk to my attorneys, which he thought wise he said, and would get back to him. He set a deadline, mighty short, and was about to hang up when I asked what price Ms. Harthorne was offering for the attempts on my life. There was a hand-over-the-phone pause and the lady came on herself.

"You've always been a fool," she said. "I shouldn't tell you this, but you're so . . . stupid, I can't resist. You took a man out into the ocean, a person with pride based on his position, and quite nearly made him cry. What did you expect?"

"Bechman?" I asked.

"Of course Bechman. Only a pompous little man like that would try to get revenge. And fail. The fool! We never should have given him access to our facilities after . . . no matter."

"Bechman was shooting at me?"

"My God, how did you ever . . . yes, Bechman. His people. All of your cheap publicity stunts were wrong."

"And him such a gray flannel type, too."

"I can only conclude the man went mad. First his ordeal in the Gulf of Mexico and we heard it *several* times and then an inability to adapt to changed circumstance."

"I had the wrong people," I said stupidly.

"Good God! Do you really suppose we cared all that much about some minor, unprovable, meaningless bank transactions? This is a big business, dealing in millions. You . . . you . . . idiot!"

"Well," I said, "anybody can make a mistake."

She hung up abruptly and I had a beer with the Evanses and told them about the offer and they were all for it.

I didn't know. It made me feel ashamed. I was a whore, perhaps, not quite this bad, but I'd never been so coldly offered a chance to whore before. Save a little face, give me a rationalization, please. I had a nightcap with the Evanses, noting happily that I was apparently back in good standing, since he was willing to drink with me again. With country good manners, they didn't harp upon my troubles or the money and we talked about fishing, the new form of cancer insurance they had purchased, and whether the redfish had recovered from last year's freeze.

Outside, Bullit charged the cat, perhaps remembering her duty and anxious to demonstrate to me that she was still on the ball dogwise. The cat fluffed up its fur, claws out, spitting, and I thought of Ms. Harthorne.

I wonder what had happened to Bechman. First they had forced him out of his job and he had focused his revenge on me. A two-time loser since I had countered with videotape. I suspect they had done something permanent, nonviolent I hoped. That was why I had been able to live recently without anybody bothering me. I felt very glad I wasn't working for Ms. Harthorne. Bechman! And I started roaring with laughter, all alone on my deck, Sir Galahad whipped up on the wrong dragon, was it too late to say, "Kings X," wait, hold everything?

32

Damn but I wanted that money. Two years' net, cash in the bank, earning interest, a two-year paid vacation. I could call it a sabbatical. It was justified, sure it was, they had taken something from me just as surely as they had stolen it and who wouldn't want the reparation?

I sat up on the deck outside the bedroom and the air was clear, a gentle southeast wind keeping me almost too cool, Bullit underneath my chair, sleeping contentedly, she had to improve her self-image with the cat but she was glad to walk back to the house with me, unscathed.

The money would buy a boat, a bigger boat, perhaps a thirty-one-foot Bertram like the one that had chased me in the Gulf, and I dreamed of fly bridges, and the sparkle of sunlight dancing among the waves, deep diesel growls, twin chrome throttles, a boat to laugh at three- to five-foot waves which now had me grimly hanging on.

For well over twenty years, I'd made a living and bought on time and I had accumulated things, most of which had gone away at their hands. I deserved the money, I really did. Of course, the things were only things and not worthy of philosophical debate, but I loved them. Potent indicators of a job fairly well done. Besides, my investments in saltwater toys, boats and rods and electronics, would be enjoyable in themselves, testimonial to the things man did well. I wanted the money.

I deserved it, that was plain.

I went back to Evans and borrowed his truck, a sleepy wife giving me a good-night hug, and I envied them their acceptance, rollers now and then so what, he chewed tobacco. It wasn't such a bad life as all that.

Evans's pickup was a massive machine, well tuned and quiet, full auto, a four-wheel-drive lever poking from the floor. Big tires, stiff springs, and shocks, a perch as high as Vince's van but much more control. I motored toward Port Lavaca and Margrit, belted in state law, Bullit riding shotgun for me, eyes bright at this unexpected nighttime excursion.

There were three places I'd thought I'd look, the not-quite-local watering holes. I avoided the shrimper bars down by the piers because they were too rough for me and, I thought, Margrit. Seven days or two weeks on a forty footer in the capricious Gulf built up more steam than a man could vent and I never fought for fun, even when young.

I drove across the long bridge, Lavaca Bay glittering in the late-night moon, water smooth, flags hanging limply. Good fishing tomorrow and I deserved the money. An old-time highway restaurant of moderate fame was on the left, now closed, and I was sad to see it gone, many fresh fried shrimp later. My first stop was an independent motel, owners local people, they must have recoiled in horror when the chain motels had come and built bigger, cleaner units down the highway from them. One response was to expand what had been an indifferent restaurant into a disco, Port Lavaca not bowing to current fashion, glitter, lights, and noise, hard-thumbing bass felt in your spine, pretty girls in shiny costumes, lots of leg, would you like a drink. I would and did and there was no Margrit and I left the change and went on to the next. The Port Lavaca cruiser went by me as I pulled out of the lot, a long look from the officer at the wheel, cage and shotgun both evident in the parking lot lights. I wouldn't want to be black and drunk and tangle with small-town cops.

She was quite evident at the next place, a restaurant/bar off the edge of the city's center, quiet family place, I thought, but Margrit and her group had run the families off, or it was too late for the kids more likely. She was at a big round table, three couples and an extra man and I guessed the extra was for her, since he was sitting with his bulky arm draped across the back of her chair.

She saw me come in and took no notice, enjoying the awkwardness. I hooked the chair out from the neighboring table and straddled it, asking, "You ready to head for the barn?"

The escort glowered at me, shiny pink cheeks and beef, cowboy hat that never saw the sun pushed back on his head, lots of pearl buttons, an incipient belly, stubby fingers, rings, and glitter.

"Howie, this is Beaumont, a man I know," she said. I would have thought I'd get better billing than that since we shared a room. I shook and he didn't try to crush my knuckles, a pleasant surprise. He was into a "lot of things, what's my game."

"I'm . . . retired," I said briefly, and he laughed. At me. I told Margrit it was time to go. "I need to talk to you."

She sniffed, an honest-to-God sniff, and tossed her

head. She was having none of it and the hopeful shrugged at me and told me the lady had made up her mind.

"She found it then?" I asked, and the other couples were quiet, small-town folks playing at the good life, always a tiny apprehensive chip on shoulders here, knowing that they were a bit behind the current, must be current, trends. They cared, that was the worst of it. Maybe they tried too hard and that was the root of the slightly out-of-focus unease that hung over the table. Better they should be what they were and quit reading glossy magazines but I didn't feel like explaining this to the audience. Things went from bad to worse and I couldn't curb my tongue, a thousand Margrit-resentments spilling forth. As I once more dug my grave with my tongue, I found a silent ally, a tan blonde lady huddled small next to her husband but smiling at my wit.

The beefy dude was having none of this, Margrit's sweet mouth a promise for later, and he wanted to get physical, waiters converging, so I got up to leave, him tagging at my side, to go outside in time-honored stupidity and there was a faint red tint at the edges of my vision, stupid woman. I refused to look at him, take the measure of his muscles and determination, and I hoped that he'd had just a bunch of drinks. We headed to the parking lot, wary, no sucker punches needed, thank you very much.

I needed him down and still quickly, his fists a deadly weapon which scared me green, and I was having none of this *shit*. I broke hard left as soon as we exited the restaurant, covey of waiters a silent escort to the door, no dishes broken here, please. I faked a run to pull him to me, rage bouncing around my consciousness to merge with fear, time slowed and vision narrowed, the last time I'd get hurt because of her, too many hurts and too much shoving, too many scars on what remained of my male pride.

Oh, I put him down, poor fellow. A wild punch landing where it should by some miracle and it's hard to fight effectively when you can't catch a breath but I had no mercy in me. The adrenaline rush was pouring through my blood and I remembered Vince talking about how to fight and hurt him in several ways simultaneously.

The one good shot he landed seemed like a hammer hitting my neck and frightened me enough to make me serious.

His friends wanted to help but they were too late and I shamed them quickly, private fight. Margrit was leaning on a car looking beautiful and her face was a mass of disgust and something I didn't want to analyze, glittering eyes and shortened breath, bulls fighting for the right to mate.

"You bitch . . ." I began.

Her words were about as bad as the fighting, green nasty smoke curling from her lips and foam flecking, she had had a bellyful of me, that was apparent and I remembered the Gold Card my antagonist had displayed on the table.

"I'll leave your stuff at Evans's," I said, and had to repeat it twice. I helped the fighter to his feet, cussing me, and it was a relief to feel the heat of honest anger, not the Margrit version which came straight from hell.

"I was stupid, I was wrong," I told him. "I'll get out of your hair. Good luck." And he looked at me, unsure, his luck was wonderful, a city vision slim and waiting, well warmed by the combat and with a few more threats and "Next times" I got out of there, beginning to feel the hurts, maybe he hit me more than I realized.

I looked at her being protective now, fussing with the Port Lavaca hero, still stunning and, in the bad light, delectable. I split in half. I was soaring, freed by circumstance and a Gold Card happening by and, oh God, what would I do. I took a step toward her and she had no eyes for me and I went to the truck and left. I turned around on the quiet streets within a mile but the group had cleared the parking lot and I couldn't face the restaurant now, so I drove out to the highway.

I couldn't turn my neck to the right at all and acid bile rose in my throat before I cleared the bridge going home. What kind of prize leaps for the next Gold Card? And more important, what kind of person competes for such?

I wasn't going to take the fucking money.

33

I HAD THE DRIVE TO VICTORIA WIRED. My pickup, a clone of Evans's, could find its way unassisted or so it seemed, often late at night had done it, a merciful God watching over, probably shaking His head— I hoped I hadn't tried His patience to the limit. I liked the place, rich farmers and ranchers, back to their real role now that the pump jacks were mostly still and the oil money less important.

My office was plywood furniture, do-it-yourself canvases on the walls, a big good color print here and there. I had built the desk and stuff by myself, a legacy from my father, joints screwed *and* glued and simple straight lines, burlap covering the surfaces to blend with the Formica tops. But it looked right and I had enough work to keep me busy, a working relationship with the editors here, a

TV spot with local talent there. In dollars there was no comparison but my Houston house had finally sold and I paid my long-suffering debts to the old agency's suppliers, so I was clean.

Probably my running buddies back in Houston laughed at me.

Or maybe they shook their heads, poor Beaumont, had a promising career once, one of us, what happened?

I caught a hell of a lot of fish and sold an outdoors story now and then, my stuff not really acceptable since I had no patience for techniques and tips. I wrote about the mullet once and the editors thought me crazy, mullet and shrimp not terribly glamorous but an essential part of the endless cycle into which I intruded now and then.

I couldn't go the cowboy route, hats with feathers and piping on the hand-sewn suits, because I was more at home on concrete and deathly afraid of horses, large dumb animals. So I bought my clothes in Dallas or Houston, three-piece suits for five days, somber colors, banker clothes. Not as somber as Bechman's but maybe an assistant vice president with high hopes. Then jeans or shorts on the weekend and I enjoyed both.

Victoria, Texas, needed a first-class ad agency.

I wrote Ms. Harthorne and told her she had no worries from me, I was through and out of it and she could forget the waivers. No reply. And it took some time to get out of the habit of making the block a couple of times with eyes on the rearview mirrors, looking for blue Fords or crazed assassins, nobody cared enough to harm me here. I found a good restaurant where they charbroiled the steaks over mesquite coals, not knowing they were in the forefront since they had always done just that. And a divorcée lady now and then, not often.

American Title Investment Group would make the news now and then, a diversification and dismantling it seemed, but there would be something similar to take its place. I didn't want to know. Attack a windmill and the sonuvabitch can kill you.

Evans and I built a boat shed, a handsome structure in my eyes, creosote poles, hand-me-downs from the phone company from Evans's connections. He supplied the engineering, displaying a surprising amount of knowledge and a stern quality-control approach, fueled by a reproving tongue. I dug the holes and carted things, held boards and hauled massive sheets of sheet iron for the roof. My boat fit nicely.

"It just goes to show you it pays to be snoopy," I said to Bullit as we made the turn onto the red gravel road into Point Lookout and my place. Then I stiffened because there was a strange car parking outside my door and a large person sitting on my outside deck, in my favorite sunset-watching chair.

Old Vince knew how to fit in, although I wasn't used to seeing him in faded jeans and had to adjust memories accordingly. I waved as I parked and Evans came out of the house with two glasses, dark brown contents, so I was glad of a replacement half gallon of whiskey on the seat.

"Down to see how the other half lives?" I asked from the top of the outside stairs, Bullit already on her back so Vince could scratch her belly. I thought of Margrit.

"R and R," he said.

We shook and hugged, awkward but well meant, and Evans announced he had the steaks and would we wander by in about an hour. Vince and I sat and watched the water, glowing a little reddish from the sun, and I asked about business. Saki had gone in the night, nobody knew where, and a citizen's group was running a petition to get him to move the club but he figured that was under control. Business was okay. He had solved "the other little problem."

I looked at him uncomprehendingly and he told me of a stakeout at the Warwick, a tailing of ole No-Neck, and a

grim bit of business, parking lot again, satisfactory conclusion. Business was okay.

"Girls and booze, how can I go wrong?" He shrugged.
"When I called, they said you were staying here alone
these days."

I shrugged and made a bad joke.

I told him of my progress, making fun of plywood furniture and tiny ads, and he shook his head. "What more
do you want?" he asked, and I couldn't think of much.

The reds were in and I told him of the grassy banks
where I'd been drifting, promised an early morning start.
He showed me bass tackle and I rigged a leader for him
and we ate too much at Evans's, Mrs. Evans going all out.
Good country food and too much of it and we did our
damnedest, Vince opening her up like a flower, most respectful and charming.

We put a cap on the night, getting his stuff stowed, and
he told me we'd have an early morning visitor, a fish-mad
fool, he said. I didn't like that much, too much intrusion
on my carefully designed privacy, but Vince was Vince
and if he wanted to bring a dozen friends, that was all
right with me.

I got up early, waking before the alarm, and went
downstairs to make a pot, the black stillness of the morning a familiar anticipatory thrill. I was silent in the quiet,
hearing some snoring sounds from Vince's room, far cry
from his hardwood floors and ten-foot ceilings, but he
seemed to enjoy it nonetheless. I could smell the marsh
smell, wet and fertile.

The glaring lights bouncing down the road caught my
attention as I sipped from the steaming mug, watching the
unfamiliar car negotiate my drive. I could see a yellow
glow from Evans's kitchen and I could see him there,
white neoprene boots and coveralls, face a little gray in
the early morning, listening to the fifty-thousand watter
out of Houston, farm news and weather reports, a country

tradition from the first broadcast, I wished I had the radio on too.

The car stopped and she got out, shorts and a halter, brown young belly, hair even shorter now, great legs, and a no-nonsense pack of duffle. She bent into the hatchback and maneuvered out two rods, red reels, strung and ready and with popping cork rigs already attached.

She stacked her stuff on the edge of the porch, leaning the rods carefully against the post.

"I understand a girl can catch a fish around this place, is that right?" she asked. And came to me and kissed, real kiss this time, hands clutching my bottom to pull me into her.

Vince said from the door, "You-all can wait until I get my fishing in, I hope."

"Just barely," Tammy said, and kissed me again.